The Goldfish Bowl

# The Goldfish Bowl

*A Jungian Novella*

David B Churchill

Pony One Dog Press
Washington, DC

# The Goldfish Bowl

© 2022 David B. Churchill

Cover art by Howard David Johnson
Book layout by Barbara Shaw

ISBN 978-1-7322882-4-9

First Edition

Published by:
Pony One Dog Press
Suite 113
1613 Harvard Street, NW
Washington, DC 20009

for J. C. Starkey

*"the better maker"*

# Chapter 1

"I'm going to skip over all the other stuff I told you before," Jason Rocketts said, "and get right to the point."

As if to signal she was listening, Donna's lips shifted the straw from the corner of her mouth to its center. But the slight wince that escaped her control seemed to suggest she retained memory of anything he'd ever told her before.

The place where they were sitting looked to have begun life as an upscale rowhouse from America's Industrial Age; but back in the day when Donna first frequented it, it had been a lesbian hang-out called "The Hungry Firkin." several generations of younger people and two or three different owners later, it still maintained that aura of desuetude it had worn in the Sixties, that indescribable something like the odor in a Goodwill Store. The bar along one wall and the booths and a few tables appeared to be historical. Nothing had changed except its name. Even some of its old clientele still hung on, but at a much reduced speed now, taking five or ten minutes, sloth-like, to negotiate the door, or to walk the length of the bar to the restrooms in the back.

What hadn't survived was its liquor license. In one of its iterations it had become an upscale coffee-shop. Now a couple of women owned it, neither of whom could make coffee. Its only claim to distinction was that it stayed open twenty-four hours a day. As a consequence, the background sounds to their voices were almost notional: a hiss of steam, a human vocable that might have been a curse, a faint vinyl warbling that was too good for this earth, woven into the silence.

A man with the look of an explorer who spent too much time out of touch with civilization and a woman with a lip-ring fit right in.

Ignoring her expression, Jason said, consciousness is One, right?" A shift in emphasis indicated which word was capitalized. "You agree with that, right?"

Even the smallest units of matter and energy were conscious, albeit in such a rudimentary form he wondered if he wasn't the first to have recognized it. But who could deny that the reactivity of matter and energy, through higher and higher levels of complexity, becomes self-aware consciousness, once they entertained the notion?

"Not only are *we* individually conscious," he went on, "but all our consciousnesses together are One consciousness. We exist in consciousness. The whole universe is conscious. We swim in consciousness. We're like angel-fish. Consciousness is a fish bowl."

*This* was something she was used to. The authoritative hyperbole. The statements flung out without explanation or excuse: consciousness is one, period. The conclusions whose premises he didn't need to rehearse because of course you were as smart as he was and already knew them.

Most people didn't.

All this passed in a flash between the two of them. They knew each other well enough to transmit volumes with the blink of an eye, including footnotes. They'd been friends more than thirty years.

"I saw three people—no, really four," he said, right to the point, as he had said he was going to do, "on a corner yesterday."

Donna repeated her straw rolling maneuver, now with a more guarded expression.

"A girl in her twenties, a middle-aged woman with a child, and an old man. Now here's the thing. The old man wouldn't approach the twenty-year-old, there's no future there. She's looking for a mate, someone to start a family with. Not going to work out."

"He wouldn't hit on the middle-aged woman either, for the same reason. She needs to finish raising her family. She needs someone who can support her. He's not going to want to get involved with someone else's kids.

"And none of them are going to want to get involved with an old man—not even to want to meet him and get to know who he is. The same with the two women with respect to each other—though the younger one might do some babysitting for the older one—but that would be about it."

"Why doncha just give Bumble a try?" she said, either teasing him or uncannily intuitive.

"That's not what's wrong with me," he said sternly. "Now listen—" He explained it again.

"They're all in the same physical space, these people. But because consciousness is One, they're also in the same consciousness bowl, like a goldfish bowl. But they can't interact with each other. They can't encounter or connect with each other. There are obviously boundaries around them. It's like the goldfish bowl has rooms in it. Each one is in his or her own room. They can see each other and talk to each other but their lives are separated from each other by something. And we can't see it. We can't see what's separating them."

'How can consciousness be divided into rooms?" she said. "What would divide them?"

Jason slapped the table. "Exactly! That's the question! How can consciousness be divided? I don't know. Maybe it's like the winds. Have you ever looked at winds? Out of the oneness that is the atmosphere, one wind blows on one tree, another blows on another tree, and the tree in the middle never stirs."

Instead of nodding enlightened, she said, "You're over-thinking things."

Jason looked at her with theatrical sadness. For a man, Occam's razor was something to clarify thinking; a woman would try to shave with it.

"Seriously," she said, "you are majorly ADHD."

He laughed. "I just thought it was an interesting idea. Consciousness divided into different rooms. People drifting past each other as if in soap-bubbles. People act like that though, don't they?"

"Maybe that explains some of *my* problems," she conceded.

This was the kind of banter he liked. The purpose of life was to laugh and have fun. He offered to buy her another iced-coffee.

She declined but laid her palm on the back of his out-stretched hand. "Don't worry, we'll figure it all out, sooner or later."

Instead of feeling heartened, he frowned. What was it she thought it was, that needed to be figured out?

EIGHT A.M. NOW and rush hour was on, forcing him to thread between the cars to get home across the grid-locked streets. Donna had fallen asleep around six. He had pulled two twenty-dollar bills and a pen from one pocket and a roll of scrap-paper from another and peeled off a piece.

> THANKS FOR PUTTING UP WITH
> ME YOUR A GOOD FRIEND I O U
> PS USE THIS TO BUY SOME
> SKITTLES FOR THE KIDS

Folding the note, Jason tucked it and one of the twenties into Donna's half-curled palm on the table, slid the other bill under the sugar-shaker for a tip, and left.

Not in this coffee-shop but in other bars and coffee-houses like it they had sat up all night back in the day, full of the ideas and prophecies of the young, croaking like bullfrogs around a pond of enchantment, until, exhausted, they had fallen out into the rays of the morning, talked out, drifting away down peace-ful and seraphic sidewalks, finally ready for sleep.

This part of the city always seemed to respond to mornings in unpredictable ways. The streets ran parallel to each other, but the canopies of oak and sycamore overhead threw a disheveled shade over them, mixing their rigor up with a preposterous chaos; except in winter, when the bareness of everything made them exceptionally dreary. Then there was the sky. Whatever the morning rush-hour was up to, the sky would always be doing the opposite: grid-lock on earth, the sky would be free as a bird; lighter traffic, the sky would be thick and low to the ground.

Under any conditions, the world was always less than expected. These rows of turrets and string-courses that the mind recognized as architecturally interesting merely looked walked on, as though nothing had a purpose except to hold up its own weight, like a sidewalk or pavement. The world lacked passion. But perhaps that was its grace. Otherwise how would you know it was real and that you were awake?

He was tired but struggling to remain buoyed by the hours he had spent with Donna. Talking, wiping at the table-top, chewing straws, toying with the ashtray, mostly not talking, then him talking again. A rare treat, considering her partner, who didn't like children, was watching the kids.

Everyone was in their own bubble, so to speak. Some bubbles contained more than one person, lovers, team-mates, families for example, all in a single bubble. Not only that, but bubbles could join and split off again, forming new groups— leaving some people alone. And as in Donna and Gina's case, there were bubbles inside bubbles.

If only he could get out of his own bubble and into a different one. Things in his own bubble had grown troubling. It now contained the story of a certain young man: in the middle of his thesis the young man gets tempted off course by an interesting cross-breeze, and never returns.

"The Influence of Something on Something in Something-Century Thought." Not his choice. His advisor suggested it. "I've been saving this subject," he'd said. "It deserves someone special to tackle it. Plus it'll open doors for you. You'll thank me some day."

He couldn't even remember what the idea was that distracted him. Probably nothing at all, something completely frivolous. Ideas probably always distracted him. This was just the first time he ever needed to *not* be distracted. For once in his life he needed to learn everything there was to know about *one thing*—and he hadn't been able to do it.

Ideas came and went in his head like the weather. He couldn't open and close himself the way he imagined others must be able to do, open to let something in, close it to keep everything else out. Some said he was lucky, he should consider it a gift. Like having perfect pitch, able to hear more vibrations than others could hear. Maybe he should embrace it.

In the meantime however he knew the only course he could follow was to continue as he had, keeping up a diary of everything he did each day, and keeping separate notebooks, one for ideas for future investigations, another for old ideas, writing them down and working them out, page after page, until a new tangent emerged, one that would lead into a whole new series of journals and notebooks.

These he saw himself working at till he died, partly an

anchor in his old age, holding him to his youth, partly in ex-piation—an atonement for the many years during which he'd stubbornly refused to accept he was just like everyone else—or-dinary.

At that moment he was passing the front of a store that ap-peared to be closed. The windows on the inside were covered with newspaper, the lights off. A sign on the outside said "Com-ing Soon"; nothing else. As he passed, the store-front suddenly lit up.

# Chapter 2

Donna followed him out to the car a few nights later when he showed up to deliver a pizza. He had no idea what she wanted but it wasn't to give him a tip. Pizza wasn't something they could afford very often but Gina earned a few paychecks and sometimes decided to splurge. Gina wouldn't have allowed her to tip him anyway, even if they did have the money.

The first cold rain of the season was in the air, patches of glitter filled with misguided lights. Donna slipped quickly into the car, her face coming at him through the lights of the dash in illuminated parts.

"Remember that note you left," she said, hardly stopping to pull out the scrap of paper he'd left that morning at the coffee-shop, "where you said you owed me one?"

He decided Donna was never more beautiful than when she needed something, which in his opinion wasn't often enough. The years seemed to have left their mark on her with a gentler hand, as a mother who straightens the hair and wipes the tears of a child.

A chivalric impulse mounted in his chest. "Yeah. Of course. What d'you need?"

At that moment the door in the building opened behind her and Gina's figure appeared. She wore her hair in the kind of cut that left her hair falling around her head like sepals on a rosebud. At that distance she looked like Tinker Bell.

As Donna turned to follow his gaze, her two younger children pushed out and stood staring beside her, bouncing and shivering. Then the youngest broke free and came skipping down the steps.

Donna rolled down the window as Riley danced across the sidewalk. In his pajamas and still with a bib around his neck, he gave a little jump and stuck his head in the car. His father's lineage had evidently waited till the last generation to put all its left-over energy into him. A sound like two animals butting heads, a noise Jason somehow interpreted as being directed at him, then the window was empty and Riley was skittering back up the steps, past the others and into the building. The older boy followed. Only Gina remained a moment longer. Her lone figure in the half-opened door stood as if in a pantomime for only one person. A neighbor struggling up the stairs with her arms full pushed past into the hallway behind her and disappeared without a glance as if to drive the point home. The world had better things to do. The door widened and narrowed again as it closed and finally Gina too disappeared.

The curtains on the window of the front apartment fluttered and pulled back as two smudges appeared behind the pane. A hand floated and waved.

"The kids know," Donna said, watching.

"Know what?" Jason asked.

She faced him again, still holding the IOU. "I need you to help me get away from Gina."

An arctic finger touched the base of his spine. Consciousness was stirring. As if he hadn't already guessed as much from the dumb-show he had just witnessed. Finally he spoke. "That's a tall order, m'lady."

"I can't live with her anymore. She's making my life miserable."

Jason crumpled the note and tossed it in the cup-holder. "I meant it more like lending you my car, for a doctor's appointment or something— "

"No, you meant it to help me, whatever I need," she insisted. "And this is what I need. Gina won't let me do anything. She won't let me out of her sight. She even gives me grief for wanting to hang out with my other friends now and then. And she definitely doesn't want me to work."

"Have you told her to back off?"

"She thinks I'm cheating on her."

"Tell her it's over then."

"I've tried. She won't listen."

"Has she threatened you?"

"Not in so many words— "

"You need someone to help you move out?"

"The apartment's in my name. It's rent controlled."

"Well, what else can I do? I can't order her to leave."

"I spent a whole night listening to you," she said starkly. "Rambling on about yourself and your crazy ideas."

"I know, I know— I'm not saying I won't help you."

She looked at the door and the front of the building again. "I better go back. She's going to be wondering what we're talking about."

"Fine. What's the plan, then?"

"I love her but I can't live with her," she said. After a moment she added. "She's too controlling."

"Tell her you need your space."

"You have no idea," she said, opening the door to go in again. "You just have no idea."

Now Jason drove again through the city's shifting lights, his car reeking with every new order of Thai and Chinese he picked up, sending his stomach into bottomless contractions of hunger. A day-old cup of coffee kept his eyes opened to consume the constellations of slow-moving traffic.

No one who knew him now wondered anymore how a candidate for a Ph.D. in philosophy at a top-rate university ended up driving for a delivery service. Once his studies shambled to their final close, the rest of his life seemed to go to pieces too. Losing that one organizing principle, no matter how shaky, pulled the rug out of everything else. His teaching jobs, his research jobs, his very ability to do organized work, to be on time, to punch a time-clock, collapsed like a house of cards.

Only the bedrock things remained, like being there for his friends. Only the bare-boned ideas, the moods, the regrets, a world that had lost its passion, remained.

The plan was this: they (meaning *he*) would tell Gina he and Donna had gotten involved and he wanted to move in with her. They had known each other a long time and they had finally succumbed to each other. He knew and liked her kids and they liked him. Gina would have to move out.

"I've never had to be alone," Donna said. "I wouldn't have been able to survive on my own. Three kids, no skills, can't stay on a budget. But I've never had to try. I've always been grateful for that. But I need to try. I think I can do it now.

"For one thing, I'm kicking Luna out," she said, speaking her oldest daughter's name bitterly. "I've put up with that girl long enough. She won't stay in school, she's not working. I'm expecting her to come home any day now and tell me she's pregnant, and I've had enough of kids. I've raised my own and that's enough. I'm not raising anyone else's.

"Riley and Buster will just have to be latch-key kids," she continued. "If I can't get subsidized day-care, they'll have to be. They can do it. They won't like it but they can do it.

"And *I* can do it," she said. "Single moms all over this city are raising more kids than I have and surviving, and I can do it too. I *want* to do it."

Donna could have always survived on her own if she'd wanted to. As she knew, single women with more children than she had did it. The city offered ample resources: day-care and pre-school, health care, food stamps and subsidized housing. It wasn't easy being poor, no one was saying that. The bureaucracy that grew like a kudzu vine to support them held them fast in its plethora of soulless and imprisoning tendrils. Only two demands were made of them: fill out forms and wait while they were processed. Most people didn't notice the lack of individuality these sacrifices accorded them. To be poor had apparently always meant being faceless.

But sometimes the issue wasn't always merely a matter of material help, an extra pay-check or help with the kids. The way Donna's eyes wavered with a sudden inability to hold his gaze seemed to indicate she already knew this. Her last words had landed firmly but a certain weakness at her brows hinted that there might be more to it, like help filling a certain void in the soul.

Jason had never been able to say no to a woman. But in actuality he had a history of bad experiences helping people out. Lending money was the worst. If someone couldn't manage their budget, it was a pretty good bet they wouldn't be able to manage it well enough to pay you back. And people who needed to borrow your car or a book or a coat, or crash on your couch, once they realized how readily you helped them, were prone to return when they needed something else. It was like feeding wild animals.

But the real alarm bells went off when he was asked to get involved in other peoples' lives—and they were going off now. Lending emotional support, being someone you could talk to, was one issue, but there was a clear line between that and trying to be an agent of change.

The plan he settled on was to talk to Gina when she was at work. She had begun taking a few night shifts covering the front desk at Wellsprings, a psychiatric hospital in the city. He would wait till around two or three in the morning, when it was quiet.

Safest way to break up with someone, he figured, outside a restaurant.

# Chapter 3

"Hey! What happened? Why didn't you call me?"

Donna's voice had a particular squeak when she was upset; her cellphone shrilled in Jason's ear now. He rolled over, shaking his head like a dog with a cricket in its ear. He struggled with the sheets to get the phone away from his head.

"How'd it go?" Donna repeated. "You were supposed to call me. I got out this morning with the kids and stayed out for a while. When I got back Gina was asleep. Did you tell her? What'd she say?"

"Sorry. I got in late."

Jason sat up, hustled to attention by the note of panicky anger rising in the voice on the phone.

"So," he said. "Actually . . . " How to phrase this? "I didn't tell her. Not yet. I went over there, but something came up."

"Something came up? What came up?" Now an even more

frustrated tone spiked the irritation. Yet a part of it almost sounded relieved.

"Yeah. Don't worry. I can't explain it," he said, fully awake now. "You got to trust me. Everything's still on. I just need another day or two."

For a long time the night before he had sat in his car across the street from the Wellspring Office, choosing and re-choosing his words as patients and staff dribbled out into the cold night and the cars on the street dwindled and condensed into rarified buses. He could see Gina at the desk inside: the lobby was a wide cove entirely open in glass to the street. She preferred the kind of jobs where she could show up in jeans and oversized tops and the night shift at a psych hospital was one of them.

Finally, after what seemed like hours since the last employee had left the building, the lobby lights went out, throwing its contents into sudden outlines and shadows imperfectly hidden by patches of illumination.

A balcony ran across the back, leading to a flight of stairs on one side, its treads discreetly lit by invisible accents. On the other side stood the desk where a swoop of Gina's hair bent over something in front of her. Between them floated a furniture of couches, tables and bayonet plants, furtively lit.

"Hey, look who's here," she said, sounding genuinely glad to see him, as she buzzed him in. "What're you doing in these parts after dark?"

The desk in front of her was covered with books, a half-eaten sandwich, a soda, as well as the usual tools of the night shift, rolodexes, dangles of keys and telephones, all lit by the same secretive light.

"I was actually going to call you," she said. "Someone's looking for you."

Jason found himself staring down at a plain white  business card.

*Robin Wyatt*
*Caspar and Caspar, Attorneys at Law*

A phone number was scrawled in pencil across the back.

"At least you don't have to worry she's pregnant," Gina said with more a smirk than friendly levity.

"What did she want?"

"Didn't say."

Another business card lay on the desk beside her. Jason reached down to take it as well. Gina quickly covered it with her hand and it vanished.

"Can I have that card too?" Jason asked.

"Nope."

"Why not? You don't need it."

"I'm saving it," she said.

"For what?"

"Oh, I don't know." Her pixie-like eyes stared at him teasingly. "A souvenir?" Her expression seemed to question whether he would believe her, making clear at the same time she didn't care—more, that it would be funnier if he did.

Jason stared at her perplexed for a moment, turning the

card he held over in his hands, as though by so doing it could be made to give up more information.

"So, did you give her my number?" he asked from under shaded lids.

"Nope."

"You gave her my address?"

"Nope. Listen—you don't have anything to worry about. I didn't tell her where to find you. I'm sure she doesn't know what you look like. Jason, you know I'll always look out for you," she said, her mirth breaking the surface now. The other card reappeared. She pretended to gnaw on it, looking up at him from under her lashes.

Again he paused, feeling his lips tightening against his teeth. Then he said, "I wonder how they got *your* address?"

"Didn't you used to get your mail at our place for a while? That summer you were living in your car? We still get mail for you all the time. Junk mail. Plus, your car's still registered at our place," she reminded him.

"Did Donna see this?"

"Nope. She wasn't home. And I didn't tell her—"

What happened next was best remembered from the safety of the sidewalk. A shout, a door slam and a thunder of running feet announced a rout of demon forms charging across the balcony and spilling down the stairs. At least three types of alarms were going mad, buzzers, klaxons, overhead warnings. An escape had been staged from an adolescent unit.

Jason wasn't even sure how he got outside. He stared

back as the whirling ape- and goat-forms besieged the desk. For a moment Gina appeared to join in their dance. Then madcap bodies hurled themselves across the lobby at the door. While the door held they seemed to be beating at the air. Then the door gave and they came running out, shoving him as they careened past.

"Let's grab him! A hostage!" someone shouted as they fled by. But nobody touched him.

It took only seconds for adults to appear and give chase down the block. The door was secured again and Gina was safe. More staff appeared and the demons were quelled. Some were lead away shrieking, others laughing and whooping. All in a night's fun—ready for the next break.

Inside, Gina appeared to be straightening up the desk. She caught sight of him and waved. Then again with both arms overhead as if at a rave.

Moments later a few more of the runaways returned, each in the grip of a staff member. As they passed, Jason heard one of the staff people say, "yeah, the police'll get the rest. Downtown, there's no place for 'em to go."

"I'M BEING SUED," he said, returning home and immediately tossing the business card in front of a woman on the couch. Lindsey Rocketts, a younger version of himself with short, bowl-cut hair, dropped the game controller she had been thumbing, flipped a black eye-patch back over her right eye-socket and took up the card. "By who?" she said.

"Your mother! Who else?"

"Mother?" she echoed.

It was close to dawn now. Jason pulled back the curtains covering the only window in the place, a plate-glass wall giving onto a space, littered now with yellowing heaps of damp leaves, between the backs of the surrounding houses. A premonitory glimmer had begun to light the bricks of which it was composed, making the space look as though like a root it had absorbed all night the moonlit contours of the Victorian rooftops above it.

The apartment itself was a long single room. A walk-in closet, advertised as a bedroom, held the mattress where Lindsey slept. A jumble of miscellaneous boxes and furniture at the far end resembled belongings heaped on a curb where an eviction had taken place, hinting at where a few pieces conventionally placed near the window had come from. A table would be pulled out for occasional meals, and extra chairs were always available for company.

"A process server is looking for me," Jason said, as though his mouth had just been scalded by a boiled cabbage. "That's her card." He returned to the door to open it for a tuxedo cat. It entered meowing loudly.

"A woman, huh?" Lindsey said. "Since when do process servers hand out business cards?"

"I don't know, but that's the only possibility I can think it could be. —Mother's suing me."

The 'Mother' in question was indeed their mother, and had a name, Gerrilynn Rocketts, no one in her family, including her husband, had ever used. The difference between the noun and the name was signaled by an almost guttural spitting out of the first syllable.

Lindsey was still looking at the card, holding it up before her good eye. "But *why?*" she said.

"All that money I borrowed for college—and never paid back. What else?" He set out four saucers, one with dry food, one with wet food, another with milk and the last with water.

"I'm confused," she said, tossing the card back. "*Did* you get served?"

"Not yet— But I'll bet that's it."

"You ran into somebody with your car," Lindsey guessed next.

"Wouldn't I know if I had? Or wouldn't my insurance company contact me?"

"Something's happened to Mother," she decided, back at her game again, dying and restarting. "You should check it out."

"I'm afraid to. Can you check it out for me?"

"I can't. I only have one eye, remember?"

"Well then there's nothing I can do except stay out of sight. Make sure this person doesn't find me. Try to figure out a way to find out what it's about, without getting caught."

He didn't mention that the person in question had left two business cards, and that Gina had the other one. Or that she was obviously holding it over his head, some kind of insurance policy of her own.

Lindsey shrugged and was speedily killed again. "Oh, drat!" This was obviously a game she hadn't played before. Her disability check allowed for a new game each month, and usually she mastered them as fast.

Jason was still watching the cat. Checking out his offerings, it turned, dissatisfied, and ran to a pile of newspapers in a corner where it relieved itself. It was foolish to think theirs was the only home it had; obviously it was being feed by any number of people on the block who also thought it was their cat. Jason had christened it 'Saoshyant' in honor of the Zoroastrian Jesus. Lindsey shortened it to 'Shay-Shay', over his objections. 'Shay-Shay' was now the only name the cat would respond to. And Lindsey didn't even like cats.

"What're *you* up to today?" Jason asked, turning away finally. His mattress leaned against a wall and he was tired. He pulled it down and began spreading blankets over it. "I gotta get some sleep, so I hope you're going to go out or be quiet."

"I'm gonna take it easy today," she said. Yesterday she had unrolled an exercise mat and accomplished a few sit-ups. "I'm probably just going to play my game for a while. I'll use the ear-buds."

Pointing her good eye at the set, she raised the controller and seemed to take aim with it.

She had lost her other eye in the same accident that killed their father, the founder of Rocketts Mortgage Company of Loveland, Ohio, leaving her not just partially blind but subject to violent seizures. Only recently had powerful new drugs that often left her drowsy and confused become available to keep the seizures in check. Because Jason Senior had been at fault, with a blood alcohol content ten times the legal limit, she had been faced with the prospect of a lifetime in a wheel-chair, not able to work and with no means of support. It had been Jason the Younger who had said to her, "you *have* to sue Dad. I know you don't want to. I don't blame you. I wouldn't want to, either. But it's not personal. It's the only way to get his insurance company to pay what you need. And you need more than what they're offering now. Because what they're offering won't even help you walk again, and you don't know how many more surgeries and other help you might need in your lifetime."

"And don't worry about Mother," he'd added; "the insurance company'll pay it. It won't come out of Mother's money. I promise."

Jason had been only half right. The award was more than twice what they'd asked for—but more than Dad's policy allowed.

His estate paid the rest.

The day the award was announced, Lindsey and Jason had sat behind Lindsey's lawyers, but for some reason Gerrilynn Rocketts had ended up behind the insurance company's lawyers, as though this was a criminal case and she the defendant. The rest of the benches in the courtroom were empty.

In the end the judgement had been reduced, so only a pittance had had to come out of the estate. Lindsey got the surgery she needed to walk again, but not enough to be able to lead a normal life. And Jason never forgot the look on his mother's face that day in the courtroom, when the impact of the verdict became clear: her masculine features hardened into a plane of pure rancor, every cheek and brow-line straining under the force of some violent suppression, and he realized then his mother had always looked like this, under her winks and flirtations, her rouge and old-woman's mascara, under her grandeur and beneficence, and especially over his father's nodding head those late nights he came home too drunk to undress himself.

In no way was that day in court the beginning of the bad blood between them. It only became known as the beginning in the unspoken shorthand of their dysfunctional psychology. It was never mentioned, even during the years she was vigorously appealing the decision, except once—when Jason had asked why she was trying so hard to reduce the amount meant for her daughter.

"So you're a lawyer now too?" Mother had shot back. The words came out as though they had been cocked in the back of her throat for a decade, though the legal tug-of-war had only been going on for a year. "This is none of your business. Don't you think you've caused enough trouble already? You've pitted your sister against me and made our life miserable."

"And don't think you can make yourself look good by taking the side of the underdog," she added. "What does anyone know about what children need in situations like this? *I* know what Lindsey needs. I'll take care of your sister from here on out. She trusts me—even if you don't. But I can't do it if I'm left with the nothing *you* had in mind for me—thank you very much. And after all I've done for you!"

Jason had spent a lot of time sitting in his car the evening before, outside the Wellsprings building, feeling somehow, almost in a state of clairvoyance, that this might have become the issue. Obviously it would have been better, now, to have worked his way through college and grad school, instead of relying on the generosity of someone else. To him it seemed now that children often mistake the generosity of their parents, considering it their due for having been brought into existence. But something greater than parents is responsible for their birth. Parents are nothing more than the vessel of one's destiny.

Mother's repayment terms had been vague, anyway; no papers were signed. Even Dad would have had something in writing. Once Mother had even hinted that if he did well, he might not have to repay anything at all.

"I don't want you to have to worry about money," she said at one point. "I want you to just concentrate on your studies. Study study study! God knows your father could have studied a little harder. Just show yourself to be a man of some account, and I'll be proud of you."

As he had sat in the car, arriving early enough to see Gina show up for her shift, and with nothing better to do, remaining parked until the last person left the building and the lobby went dark, he had passed the time watching the only thing of beauty in the world at that moment, the sun going down in his rearview mirror.

Sunset had not always been the saddest part of the day. So long ago, it now seemed, it had been what the morning was for some people now, a time of new energies, new changes; a morning in reverse. Sunset was the beginning of night and night was the time when his day began: concerts, clubs, the endless peregrinations in search of connections, somewhere to score, people going to New York or L.A. and coming back with new stories to tell, news of other friends who had gone and might return any day now or might never return. The lights of bars and cafes seemed to be the only lights that mattered, and everyone's eyes were brighter in those lights. The things people had to say were always more trenchant and passionate; even the placement of a certain drunk on a park bench seemed to be full of sub-liminal meanings. One felt even the silent figures on monuments looked down and spoke to them.

Now sunsets were the autumns of the day. The words of that German poet who said of the autumn, "those who are alone now will always be alone" recurred at the close of every day: that what hadn't gotten done that day, would never get done. One had to work harder now to round up an old friend for a drink or a cup of coffee. Worst of all, nobody wanted to talk. No one had anything left to say.

Yet as he watched that day's sun going down now, he couldn't help but think what a vision to look at it was, what a changing palette of colors. And because the world was always only beautiful in pieces, what a waste of beauty it was. One couldn't look at it and feel transformed because the world that produced it couldn't see it and didn't care. Beauty was like a mirror in a jigsaw puzzle, it's contours fit but it wasn't part of the picture. What it was a part of was a mystery.

It was like the goldfish bowl of consciousness. Like con-sciousness itself, the world was broken into pieces. The light that flared from a thousand windows, though within the same space, was no longer connected to the rising or setting of any-thing that reflected in them; the rising or setting sun and the gleam of its reflections were merely simultaneous events, acausal synchronicities.

If you can stand at the lip of a cataract, like Niagara Falls, right where the water tears into shreds as it drops into free-fall, and not feel the water roaring through your own veins, feel yourself being rushed into free-fall with it, it's because the world has been separated into parts, and not all parts are available. Its passion was missing.

# Chapter 4

Donna called back later to tell him Gina would be at a house concert that night. As he finished writing down the address, she said, "Don't let me down again. My nerves can't take it. Gina's acting all lovey dovey and that means she's upset about something. She always gets like that just before all hell breaks loose. I'm walking on egg-shells. And the kids are getting harder to control, they're upset too."

"Don't worry. I'll take care of it tonight. But," he added, "if the situation is this bad now, what's going to happen when I tell her I'm moving in? Isn't it going to get worse?"

"I'm going to tell her you're forcing me to do it."

"She's gonna believe that?"

"She knows how weak I am."

Okay then, he thought. Visions of a vengeful Tinker Bell coming at him while he slept flitted through his head. "Thanks for the heads up."

He flipped the cell-phone off and tried to think for a while. Great ideas always came to him unbidden, but strangely, not when he needed one. His idea muse was conflict adverse, it appeared.

And as if all this wasn't enough, there was also the threat of Gina's outing him to whoever it was who was looking for him, on behalf of a law firm. Lindsey's comment that process-servers usually don't hand out business cards reassured him somewhat, so maybe he wasn't being sued—but what else could his mother want? That she would hire a law firm to track him down for? It was almost more worrisome than thinking he *was* being sued.

If this were some mythological age in which they were living, this intrusion in his life would be a call, a summons to an adventure—but the time was today and he was no knight. It could still happen perhaps that one might get a call from a lawyer's office to tell him they had won the lottery, but today's world held far more unknown dangers than pleasant surprises.

Maybe she's died he thought, and left me and Lindsey a fortune.

He checked himself. Every time anyone's wished her dead, it seems to give her new life.

But one could owe back taxes that had been sent to a collection agency, one could be contacted—erroneously or not—for child support, one could have had one's identity stolen, on the hook for millions in fraudulent charges. The list could go on. Fear of the unknown seemed to increase algebraically with the number of unknowns.

TRAFFIC HAD DIED DOWN and the early dusk was settling quietly over the streets as Jason steered toward the address Donna had given him. Different periods of history had been quilted into the city's physical structure, and he soon found himself in a period unfamiliar to him. Small streets lined with accordions of house fronts alternated with larger alleys that bore their own names: 'Milly's Alley' and 'Comfort Alley.' The life of this neighborhood lay behind its front doors and windows; darkling glimpses of city gardens, workshops and warehouses greeted his eyes as he tried to peer behind them. He knew he was getting close when parking spaces grew scare and more people appeared on the sidewalks, all heading the same direction.

The house itself, as if in keeping with the obscurity of the whole neighborhood, seemed to crouch behind a parti-colored glow that illuminated the street and the people on the sidewalk and lounging on its steps. Strings of Christmas lights had been strung along every cornice and barge-board and were wound around the railings and columns on the porch. Some of the strings on the windows and roofline blinked on and off, giving the house a winking jocularity, like a roadside whorehouse.

House concerts belonged to a different set of people than Jason normally ran with. One did not host rock bands in people's houses. These performers were what had once been called folk singers back in the day, but since then had up-graded themselves to "singer-songwriters." It seemed any de-sire to celebrate the lives of working-class Americans of the Depression era and earlier had been subsumed in a flood of identical-sounding laments on subjects like ghosting, one-night stands, racial inequality and the multiplying varieties of non-heteronormative sexuality.

But as Jason edged through the throng on the steps and across the porch to the opened door, he heard a crystalline voice singing something he was familiar with:

*If I were*
*a tiny sparrow,*
*and I had wings*
*and I could fly,*

*I'd fly away*
*to my own true lover,*
*and all he'd ask*
*I would deny.*

As if interpreting the flight-path itself, the voice lost its limpid altitude on the second verse, which was sung with such a throaty plaintiveness that Jason shuddered. Definitely not the kind of song you'd hear today. Today's songs always seemed overly explicit, afraid of leaving anything to their listeners' imaginations, but true life couldn't always be made to rhyme.

The same colors splashed the floor and walls inside, sprinkling down from more bulbs strung on the molding, blinking like linear disco balls. The house was bare except for a few chairs and tables in some of the rooms. The tables were covered with bottles around which a mostly older crowd of bearded and pony-tailed men gathered, sipping the different colored nectars from paper cups. The lights cast restless motions on their milling forms, giving them a jerky, uncontrolled existence. The majority of chairs looked to have been dragged into what might have been the dining room. Here the overhead fixtures were on, giving the space a starkly unflattering brightness. At the far end, a woman with a guitar stood alone. She wore jeans and boots, a simple blouse, and one of the braids of her hair that she tried from time to time to dislodge with a jerk of her shoulder, had slipped down and hung over one eye. The fingers that were unemployed on either hand, the one over the sound-hole as well as the one on the fretboard, stuck out as though the guitar was a tea-cup.

Her voice undulated so bitter-sweetly it seemed to be coming not from her but from some mountain hollow in another dimension, replete with both mountain streams and the scent of wildflowers. Jason gladly would have joined the throng at her feet, floating with her audience into that other realm.

He also thought how unfortunate it was to be on a mission, and such an unpleasant one, at such a longing and un-looked-for moment, when you just wanted to forget yourself and listen.

As he was coming back down from looking around up-stairs, where more people appeared to be standing around oblivious to the concert below, with still no sight of Gina, he had just about made up his mind to return to the concert when a familiar voice cut against him like an invisible wire, bringing him up with a jolt.

"Jason!" Gina cried. "What're you doing here?"

She stood in front of him leaning on a tall good-looking woman, whose arms, interlaced with hers, appeared to be the only things holding her up. The stranger had dressed as though for a night-club, a form-fitting dress that ended above the knees; Gina was herself in jeans and a t-shirt. A winged skull with snakes emblazoned the front, circled by the words, 'Existentialist Philosophers from Hell.'

"So," he said, quickly reading her shirt while trying not to focus too long on the shape of the breasts underneath it, "this is what you're up to when Donna's not around, eh?"

Gina untangled herself and gave her companion a shove. "Get lost, Sweetie. I'll catch up with you later."

With her eyes like uncut agates staring up at him out of their swarm of freckles, she pulled him down the last step and now roped her arms around him, leaning heavily on his neck. Gestures that consistently seemed to miss their mark suggested a level of inebriation.

"Hey," she said, grinning with over-abundant interest. "Didja call that number yet?

"Want me to call for ya?" she teased when he shook his head. "I'll call him up. We're buddies, ya know. We had a good talk."

"*Him?*" he repeated, remembering her comment that 'at least *she* wasn't pregnant. "I thought you said he was a she?"

Gina stared at him blankly. Then suddenly delight creased over her face. "He, she—what's the difference," she laughed, too pleased with her herself to say more. "At least you don't have to worry about *that*."

"No, I don't want you to call him," he said.

"Hey, you really don't want this guy to find  you, do you?"

"Maybe, maybe not," he said, not wanting to confirm or deny anything.

"Some kind of legal trouble, huh?"

"I didn't say that."

"If I were you, I'd want to know what was going on."

"Well, you're not me."

"No prob. I'm not going to call him. Who said I was going to call him? I'm looking out for you. We're taking care of each other, right?"

He grunted uncertainly as she reached for a better hold on his arm. That was when she saw the bandage covering the back of his hand.

"Whoa! What happened here, matey?" she said, her touch sweaty but surprisingly gentle as she maneuvered his hand to inspect it.

He had been on the couch with Saoshyant that afternoon, looking at the animal's long whiskers and bushy tail, and especially his sedate, leonine face. Suddenly his hands curled in a desire to get hold of him and feel his fur on his palms.

"Here, Shay-shay," he called, "come here, kitty."

The animal looked at him, blinked, looked away. The end of his tail twitched.

Finally Jason got up, took a page from the morning newspaper and spread it on the couch beside himself. Within five minutes Saoshyant got up came over and sat on it.

The next few events happened so quickly he wouldn't

have remembered them if it weren't for the bandage on his hand.

The contours of Saoshyant's cheeks and ears suddenly became a thorn-bush with teeth. Patiently Jason extracted his hand. "You ungrateful animal," he said. "Did you forget who feeds you?"

Saoshyant moved away, then in one consecutive blur whirled back. The knuckles of Jason's hand unzipped and the crimson stuff of his insides beaded up, then began trickling down his wrist.

Catching him again, Jason tucked him quickly into the crook of his elbow and stood up. "I know what's wrong with you. You're still too wild. Not tame enough yet. You need more petting." With the cat's paws and teeth safely positioned, he massaged the thick cheeks and throat and played with those velvety, aerodynamic ears again. "That's right, I gotta love you up more. You're definitely asking for more attention."

"Well, let me tell ya something," Gina said when she heard what had happened. "If that gets infected, you're gonna want to get it looked at. Also get a tetanus shot. But be careful what you tell 'em about where ya got it. A lot of people are required by law to report animal bites, and if you're not careful, the next thing you know, animal control'll be at your door. Take that little kitty of yours into custody.

"Here, I wanna talk to you," she said abruptly, pulling him by the arm now. As they passed one of the tables with refreshments on it she grabbed a bottle, then led him into a room with relatively few people and sank down against a wall, pulling him with her. "Whew, I'm tired."

She upended the bottle over her lips, swallowed and gasped. "Agh! What is this?" and stared at the label. "Sherry? What sucker brought this?!" She sent it rolling across the floor and with vehement spitting noises wiped her tongue on her sleeve.

Jason was beginning to wonder if he should proceed with the plan after all. Gina's didn't look capable of remembering anything in the morning. Even if she remembered, would it be fair? One didn't kick people when they were down.

Suddenly she looked up at him and her face was like a pebbled path where rain was falling. "Oh god I love her so much!" she cried.

# Chapter 5

Jason worked an arm around Gina's shoulders and held her till the crying subsided. A small stampede of applause broke out in nearby room and the number of people around them increased, but nobody noticed them. Finally Gina wiped her eyes on his shirt-front. Without looking up said calmly, "Donna's leaving me."

Jason fought a desire to react. It would be easier to play ignorant if his body didn't give him away.

"Why do you say that?"

"Because I know. Women know things like that."

As if men didn't know things like that too, Jason thought.

"I'm too controlling," she said. "I know I am. You don't need to tell me that."

Jason said nothing. The idea of trying to broker a reconciliation between these two women suddenly came to him. It was a line he didn't want to cross, but they still loved each other, that was obvious. Rather than trying to help them separate, why not see if he could help bring them closer?

"You don't think I'm too controlling?" Gina asked, looking up at him finally.

"You can be," he allowed.

"I want to change," she said. "I want to be a better person. For Donna. I want to be more like a loving man to her, not like a, a, a . . . " She seemed to struggle, not for the right word, but for something more, " . . . *an angry woman.*"

The hum of a bow on violin strings sounded and the music started again. Immediately the chatter of a banjo joined in and a medley of voices arose like a flight of musical birds. Were they singing 'Shady Grove'? Jason couldn't tell. People began drifting toward the song and soon they were along again.

"Jason, we look out for each other, don't we?" she said. "Teach me how to be more like a man. Let's start dating. I'll be the woman and you be the man. I'll take notes."

"No," he said. "That doesn't sound right."

She swung out from his arm and pushed her face close to his. "I'm serious! I mean it! I need it! You're the only man I don't hate. You have to help me!"

"We don't need to date for me to help you."

"Well, help me then. What do I need to do? Speak, oh masculine one."

"You're mocking me."

"No! I'm serious!" She grabbed him by the collar. "Look me in the eyes. I'm a fucked up dyke. I don't want to run Donna life, I want to take care of her. Tell me!"

"This is weird," he said. "Donna doesn't like men, she likes women. Wouldn't you rather be more like a woman?"

"I am a woman."

"Or, like, a *different* woman?"

"Donna likes men *and* woman," she said. "I could be a man in a woman's body. She'd have the best of both worlds."

"Alright, fine," he said. "I'll give you some pointers."

She stood and pulled him up with her. "Let's start now."

"How 'bout we start when you're sober?"

"I'm sober now. I sober up fast. Come on! What do I do?"

They were holding hands now; their hands, almost independently and unnoticed by them, began contending to grip or be gripped.

"Well, for one thing," he said, "men and women aren't really that much different."

"Bullshit," she said.

"Like, if a man and woman are going someplace together, the woman will be talking or letting her mind wander while the man's mind will usually be two or three clicks up the road, wondering what's around the next corner. But some women are like that too."

"Gotcha. What else?"

"Well, I dunno, like rough-housing . . . "

"Rough-housing!" she exclaimed. "What's that?"

"Didn't you have any brothers when you were growing up?"

"No. What's rough-housing?"

"Well, for one thing, what I'm talking about is not the kind of rough-housing you see in locker rooms. The kind of horse-play you see between couples— "

"Horse-play!" she cried. "How d'you do that? Show me!"

They circled each other in a kind of dance while Jason hesitated a moment. Applause floated in from the throng around the performers in the dining-room. Finally he said, "Are you ticklish?"

Gina's eyes began a series of not-so-subtle transformations that would quickly overtake her. "Just try it," she said warningly.

"Oh, so you're *not* ticklish," he said, pulling her closer, his tone anything but reassuring. "I know you. Tickling doesn't bother you at all."

At this, one of his hands was already in her armpit, causing Gina to jerk wildly away. A woman would often let out a shriek at this point, but Gina's lips were clenched. Jason persisted.

"Come 'ere. You're no girly-girl," he teased. "You don't have a ticklish bone in your body. Let's check some!"

They were Indian-wrestling now, Gina's arms rigid, her grip iron-willed as she struggled to keep his hands away from her body.

"Let's check that ole tummy-bone," he cried, undaunted, a hand momentarily breaking free.

Gina kicked and Jason danced back. They were fighting now but neither seemed to know about what. Without a motive, it was hard to know exactly what they *were* doing, playing, exercising, practicing a dance routine. They ended up just continuing to do it.

In a situation like this a man's tactic is usually to try to hold both of the woman's hands with one of his, leaving his other hand free. On the first try, Gina bit him.

"Ow! Tryin' to tell me you don't know what rough-housing is! You're a regular rough-neck!"

At his second try he got another hand on her ribs, fingers not even moving. Gina dug her nails into the hand she still held, ripping the bandage off. Blood spurted.

Now Jason broke away, blood and pain unleashed from his wounded knuckles. "You little vixen!" he said, hurling the epithet into her panting face.

"You were trying to rape me!" she cried.

"Jesus Christ! You *are* a bitch. I'm outa here."

He backed toward the door, cradling his knuckles. They were alone in the room. The music started up again where the concert was still proceeding. Gina darted after him.

"No! Don't go! Don't leave me!"

"What the fuck," he said. "Get away from me!"

A man who was passing in the hall stuck his head in the doorway. "Hey, play nice now, okay?"

"No, please," Gina said, as the man disappeared again. "I'm sorry— I'm sorry, I'm sorry, I'm sorry," she repeated five or six times.

She tried to grab for the hand that was bleeding. He kept it out of reach.

"Let me kiss it," she begged. "I can fix the bandage. Let me make it better."

He relented and let her take his hand. She wiped the blood with the hem of her t-shirt. The bandage fell off. She clapped it back on and placed his free hand on top of it.

"You have to hold it."

Jason was still trying to make sense of what happened. They had been like two adult cats who start off playing and soon get the fur flying. When did it get so serious?

"Well, I better get going," he said. He lifted the bandage, looked at the scratch and set the bandage back. "I better get home and take care of his."

"Are you mad at me?"

He managed a faint smile. "No. Of course not. We both just got worked up."

"Can I give you a hug?"

"Sure."

She hugged him on tiptoes and kissed the bandage on his hand. "I'm sorry."

"I know. Not your fault."

"You're not going to give up on me, are you?"

"Of course not," he said, moving toward the door.

"We're gonna give it another try?"

"Sure. Soon as I get this fixed."

"You know I really like you," she said.

"Lucky me," he said. "Hey," he said, "go find that girl-friend of yours."

"Okay, but we got a date, right? Don't forget."

"Don't worry—."

"Mum's the word," she said, zipping her lips.

"Gotcha. Go find your friend. See if you can tickle her up a little. Consider it your homework."

"Good idea," she said, the old pixie light returning to her face. "I will. I'll try it out on her . . . "

# Chapter 6

I have to figure this out Jason thought as he drove home that night, steering through the city for the most part with one hand. With Gina holding on to that other business card, it was indeed as if he were already one-handed, one hand tied behind his back.

Hanging out with Gina behind Donna's back was a bad idea. Doing something to help them was a good idea though. Despite the fact that Gina often didn't seem to like him, he had never liked the idea of being instrumental in breaking them up. Donna wanted to make it on her own, but he was pretty sure it didn't mean she wanted to be alone. She attracted people; that was her gift, just like attracting bombastic ideas was his gift.

The chance to play a constructive role in the relationship between his friends had come to him the way the rest of his ideas came, out of the blue. Red lights were flashing and sirens going off, but the fact that Gina could be so antagonistic toward him only made it more necessary. From time to time she would blame one of Donna's children on him—whichever one was giving trouble at the time, as though they'd had a fling and now Donna wouldn't admit to it. Donna's ever having liked any man in her past seemed like a betrayal of trust. Continuing with the plan would only confirm that.

He liked and admired Donna, was in awe of her artistic side, including her taste in people and objects, so why shouldn't he like Gina too? Donna liked her and found her interesting, and indeed they seemed perfect together, Gina's flair for the dramatic, her mordant wit, her tough-guy insouciance, her style with scarves and sweaters was the perfect accent, like red against green, for Donna's gray-eyed reserve.

First stop that night, before even re-bandaging his hand, was at Donna's. He knew Gina wouldn't be there; he'd left her at the concert, hooked up with her friend again. He needed to update Donna face-to-face, no more apologetic phone calls.

Donna met him at the door in her painting clothes, splattered jeans and an over-large shirt, hair bun-rolled on the top of her head. You knew she meant business because the lip-ring was gone. A smear of mother-of-pearl on one cheek was like half-finished war-paint.

"Mission accomplished?" she whispered.

"Nope."

She mouthed the word '*What?*' punctuating it with an incredulous twist of her body.

"She was tight as a peep," he said; it was an old joke: he

never lost an opportunity to deploy it with Donna. She appeared to be the only one who knew the response.

"I don't care if she was Titus Andronicus! What'd that have to do with anything?"

"What if she got violent? I don't know how she acts when she's drunk."

"She's a weepy drunk. You missed the perfect opportunity."

"Do you mind if I come in," he said, pushing past her. "I got a flesh wound needs tending to."

"Now I suppose you'll tell me she inflicted *that* on you as well?"

The door opened directly into their hall. Donna followed him toward its end, bright with all the lights on. The boys were asleep in front of TV which was still blaring away. Donna turned it off in passing, the sudden cessation of sound stirring a grudging response from the slumbering forms, as though someone had prodded their sleep with a pole.

The kitchen was a large room with space for a breakfast nook. Here a rickety table held a profusion of tubes of paint, cans of turpentine and linseed oil and piles of rags. A canvas was set up under the overhead light where Donna had evidently begun another work: its surface showed swirls of charcoal that from a distance could have been a face. Other canvases had been propped up against the windows to dry, a confusing montage of more faces, children in different activities, portraits of herself and possibly Gina; the jabs and spits of color made them difficult to identify.

Another stack of canvases, painted surfaces turned to the wall, were waiting to be recycled, their paint scraped off, their surfaces prepared for new strokes of paint, more attempts at the same elusive subjects. To his eye, the stack seemed larger every time he saw it.

Donna's older, youthful work decorated the hall they had just traversed, hidden now by its darkness. Jason knew most of the older canvases by heart: an empty chair on a porch, an empty window looking out on an suburban street, glass bottles on a shelf; in all the styles she had experimented with: pop art, feminist art, formalism, colorism, all the other "isms" of the art world he couldn't remember.

To walk down the hall in the daytime, then to enter the kitchen and see Donna's latest works was like walking from the daylight into a cave. It just wasn't the lack of color in her current work, there seemed to be a lack of vitality, a lack of enthusiasm. Truly good art says "Look at me!" Donna's latest works seemed to almost apologize for themselves, to seek the shadows of corners and niches out of the reach of the light, to almost turn their backs on you.

The most striking quality her art-school work had was depth, the feeling of space, sunlit volumes so lucid they could have filled fishbowls; chairs sat on porches wide enough to walk on, stands of irises with room to blow in the wind, even splashes of shade on lawns that looked deep enough to actually be refreshing. The worst thing now was that, except for a few on the walls in other rooms, the majority of what Jason thought of as her best work was forced to compete for attention along a hall where there was barely enough room to stand back and admire them, the "Look at me" of each one shut up in its own dim prison.

"So what's your excuse this time?" Donna said as Jason grabbed a roll of paper-towels from the counter, not bothering to whisper anymore.

"I told you. Gina was drunk."

"God, Jason, you have no idea," she said. She wearily untangled a rag from the pile on the table and tossed it to him.

"But this whole situation is ridiculous. I know you too still love each other."

"Don't start that on me now. I know what you're trying to do."

"Do you still love her or not?"

"I can't live with her!" she exclaimed. "I told you that!"

"But what if you *could* live with her?"

"What if you could just do a simple little favor once in your life?" she countered.

"She wants to change. She asked me to help her be a better person for you."

"She was drunk!"

"She wants to hang out with me so I can show her."

"Perfect! *That's* a solution!"

"I didn't say I wanted to hang out with her. I just think it's sweet."

"No? Well, if she starts dating you, I won't need help throwing her out. It'll the perfect excuse! But it won't be too good for you, because I'll never talk to you again. And that's a promise!"

She paused. Distant sirens and the bark of a dog, the clatter of trash cans leaked into the silence. When she spoke again it was with the fatigue of resignation.

"Here's the thing," she said. "I got a job offer, see? Coffee-shop in a good hotel downtown. Friend of mine works there." She took the hand that he was clumsily trying to manage a one-handed wrap and wound the rag around it.

"Is that clean?" he asked.

"Clean enough," she said.

"It smells like turpentine."

"Everything in here smells like turpentine."

Except her. He hadn't stood this close to her in years. There was a pleasing floral and fresh biscuit aroma about her, as though she'd been baking something.

"I got this job offer," she repeated, tying the ends of the rag. "I told Gina about it. She said if I started working she'd show up and make a scene and get me fired. Well, guess what," she said, suddenly yanking the ends tight, throwing Jason into a wincing crouch. "I took the job." She turned away, dusting the exertion from her hands. "I start tomorrow."

"You know what," Jason said in a controlled tone, bandaged hand hiding itself in his armpit, "that really *hurt* goddamit."

"You wanna know what hurts, Jason?"

"I don't care what hurts!"

"Friends you can't count on."

"Why didn't you *tell* me?"

"I didn't think I had to."

"It woulda been nice!"

"I don't know what I'm going to do now," she said. "How would it look if I just called up and said hey, I changed my mind I'm not coming in, and they're short-staffed and counting on me?"

The harsh overhead light glimmered in the bottoms of her eyes. She turned away and began sorting the paints on the table, and the rags, moving them around with a resistant intensity.

"What d'you think?" she said finally, pulling the easel propped up on the table around into the light, and stepping back from it, wiping her hands close enough to her face to be wiping her cheeks. "It's going to be a portrait of Luna. I kicked her out yesterday.

THE WALKWAY through the houses to his front door seemed to climb straight up a mountain. Too late to wish she'd told him about the job sooner. The meaning of his life never felt closer and never more inscrutable. He had climbed so far and could almost see it on the next ledge above him, the last ledge, the top of whatever it was he was climbing, and he was spent. Limbs that had spent the last forty years wedded to rock surfaces could move no more.

Of course the curtain to the front window had not been drawn. The little aperture between houses that was their front yard was bathed in light. Everything inside was laid out for the world to inspect, Lindsey at the kitchen, moving bowls around, Saoshyant sitting at the door, waiting to be let out, their lawn-sale hoard of belongings piled up in the back.

"Lindsey, I need your help tonight," he said, closing the door behind him and pulling the curtain. "Nothing big, just make a phone call for me."

He was writing the phone number from the back of the

mysterious business card on a piece of newspaper when a pair of thumps sounded from the door he had just closed.

A girl covered with tattoos and in a pair of brogans stood there.

"I need to crash at your place a few days," Luna Redland said. She ruffled impatiently at a plaid skirt so short it barely curtained her groin.

"Ah, Luna. Need a place to stay, huh? Well . . . "

"Mom said you'd say no." Luna brushed past him and threw herself on the couch. As Lindsey approached with a bowl of cereal, she said, "hey, who's the one-eyed bitch?"

"That so-called 'one-eyed bitch' is my sister," Jason said, hackles rising. "Lindsey, this is my friend Donna Meadow's daughter, Luna. You've met Donna, haven't you?"

"I love that eye-patch," Luna said. "Where can I get one?

"I have a few extra," Lindsey said, joining her with the cereal. "I can give you one."

"Sweet! Got anything to eat? I'm starving."

"Help yourself," Lindsey said.

"Yeah, help yourself," Jason said, deciding to be philosophical about eventualities that were obviously not in his control. "Anyway, I have to go out again," he added, "so you girls behave yourselves."

"What did you need me to do tonight?" Lindsey called as he headed toward the pile of magical belongings in the back.

"Call me," he said, "when I'm in the car."

From the kitchen came a litany of questions in Luna's grating accent. "Where's the almond milk? How come you don't have any almond milk? Do you have any oat milk?

What kind of place is this? Don't you have anything but Fruit Loops around here?"

AN HOUR LATER Jason stood in the shine of a popular downtown 7-Eleven, a Big Gulp cup in one hand with a few coins in it and a bottle of cough medicine in a paper bag in the other, blending in with the rest of the men who called that street corner home. The secret to being homeless he had decided was not having any underwear; so as a result he had appeared in a double-breasted pin-stripe suit several sizes too large, without anything on underneath, an Adidas on one foot and a Keds on the other, without socks, and a bombardier cap, *sans* goggles but with the ear flaps and strap hanging down. The weather report had called for frost that night. He was already cold.

All he had asked Lindsey to do, when she called, was to call the number he had written down and left for her on the kitchen counter. It was the number from the back of Robin Wyatt of Caspar and Caspar's business card. "Tell him if he wants to find me," he'd said, "to come to the downtown 7-Eleven. Tell him a friend of Jason's hangs out there who knows where he is. Tell him to look for a guy in a bombardier's cap."

The plan was to ask for a few bucks in exchange for information on Jason Rocketts, whom he would pretend to know, in the hopes that this Robin Wyatt would be more talkative in front of a homeless man than he would be with someone else. To that end he would be a garrulous drunk with an inquisitive disposition; if he could pull it off, Robin Wyatt would never realize this nosey old fool was holding out on him, until he too got the information he wanted, while giving out nothing but nonsense in return.

But before going out, Jason had stood staring at the pile of junk in the back of their studio apartment. The pile was like that ancient village in France where the Celts, rampaging through Europe, had parked their baggage-wagons, never to return. Almost nothing in the pile belonged to Jason or Lindsey, except the notebooks and journals in boxes stacked neatly against the wall. Everything else, televisions and electronics, tables and chairs, couches and bedsteads, musical instruments, suitcases full of clothes, boxes of pots and pans, stuffed animals, costume jewelry and of course books and more books, had been accepted for safekeeping from various friends over the years, some facing eviction, some leaving for distant lands, expecting to return, but who never had.

Jason needed a disguise. He originally envisioned meeting Robin Wyatt in a bar, but what would prevent Robin Wyatt from guessing who he was unless he went as a woman, and he doubted he could be a very convincing woman. He poked around among the suitcases and bags full of clothes while the minutes ticked by, casting about for another idea. Finally he spied the dark, double-breasted suit and recalled that homeless man had shuffled past him on the street in just such a suit not long ago. No matter it proved a little too big for him. Wouldn't it be a hoot if the other homeless man was at the 7-Eleven too?

"I go to confront the beast," he informed Lindsey, giving her his instructions and about to hang up.

"Good luck," she replied, no questions asked. "–Oh, I had a dream last night!"

"About what?" He had already parked but was in no particular hurry. While she talked he hid his wallet and car keys in a compartment behind the glove box. No one who drives for a living and keeps money in their car can survive without a secret compartment.

"Yeah, I had a dream," she said excitedly. "I dreamed about Dad. First time. I never dreamed about him before. We were riding in a car. It was a beautiful day. He gave me a Twizzler."

"I thought you didn't like Twizzlers."

"I don't, but this was a good Twizzler. It was a nice dream. It made me happy."

Lindsey and he were opposites evidently. He couldn't remember ever dreaming about Mother and she usually never dreamed about Dad. She hadn't been in a car since the accident, either. Bus, plane, train, just so long as it wasn't a car.

Lindsey had always been the good kid. Growing up, she'd been Mother's little shadow, as much as Mother would allow. The accident changed all that. It took her so long to recover, to regain even a semblance of her health, that she seemed to have forgotten who she was. With no memory of the accident or the weeks immediately after, she seemed to have returned out of nothingness, her past life in pieces, posters on her walls, photos in yearbooks, trophies and ribbons in her bookcase. Or was afraid of who she'd been. You couldn't get her near a car. She couldn't, or wouldn't, catch up at school, where before she had excelled. Things she learned wouldn't stay in her head. She avoided her friends.

Now she just seemed happy to have a place to live where the world couldn't get her again.

Jason, on the other hand, had always been a trouble maker. Tossing his cellphone in the compartment with his wallet and car-keys and closing it, he got out, making sure no one was around. The 7-Eleven was just around the corner.

But as he walked toward the island of light at the bottom of the canyon of buildings, a heaviness fell over him, slowing his step. Gina was blackmailing him. Breaking her power would be good for him, but it would do nothing for Donna. All he had to do was find out what this Caspar and Caspar thing was about, and he would know what he was up against, but preventing Gina from forcing him to date her— or whatever else she had in mind—would leave Donna alone, still in her grip.

Donna was a good and long-lasting friend. He loved her almost as much as he had loved any woman in his life, and he had failed her. With her job starting tomorrow, and Gina, if she was still awake, immersed somewhere in her friends, there was no way he could do what Donna had asked of him now. It was a bitter piece of self-knowledge to have to absorb. But he would make it up to her. If it took the rest of his life, he would make it up.

# Chapter 7

"Jason? Jason Rocketts? Is that you?"

Jason turned at the sound of his name. A well-dressed man and a woman were standing in front of him, garishly lit by the store window as if they were actors in the flood-lights of a stage. The man looked distantly familiar.

"Hey! It's me, Brad. Bradley Baker. Don't you recognize me?"

Take a scrawny adolescent with a buzz-cut, thin the hair, add thirty pounds and a business suit and you would have had the man who stood in front of him now, extending his hand.

"Yeah, it's me, yer ol' buddy," he said, "and this is my wife, Moira," indicating the woman beside him; "I don't know if you knew her. She was a year behind us. She was a cheer-leader. Honey—, this is Jason Rocketts. I'm sure you remember him. We were on the football team together. He use to screw up all our games," he added with easy-going familiarity.

Jason allowed his hand to be grasped in mortified stu-
pefaction, suddenly aware of how he must look. Brad's grip
was full and moist; the hand his wife offered used only two
fingers to shake his index finger.

He had been leaning against the window observing the
people going in and coming out, watching for anyone who
looked like they might work for a law firm, or more precisely,
for anyone who looked like they might be looking for him.
He'd seen the suburban couple go in and return, but had ig-
nored them. At that moment one of the drunks loitering next
to him vomited, not even bother to turn his head away, but
just bent over and heaved onto the sidewalk between his feet.
The vomit splashed, leaving Jason practically standing in it.

I *knew* better than to get involved in other peoples' rela-
tionships he thought, trying to resist the urge to blame this
on Donna. Her and her problems with Gina! But a voice in
his head was screaming NO MORE EXCEPTIONS.

"So, are you on some kind of stake-out?" Brad queried.
"Jeez, hope we're not blowing your cover."

"Honey, he's homeless," Moira said.

"Whatta ya talkin' about. This is the guy voted most
likely to succeed three years in a row."

Four years actually, Jason thought.

"Doing research for some kind of project, eh?" Brad
said. "Going undercover?"

Jason mumbled something in reply. If he denied what
they were seeing, he ran the risk of sounding loony as well.
Trying to explain the real reason he was hanging out with the
drunks dressed like a homeless person and covered with vomit

might have sounded even loonier.

"Honey," Moira insisted, "smell him. He's homeless."

"Yeah, I can see why you'd think that," he finally got out.

The expression on Brad's face slowly took on a different dimension. At the same moment a violent shiver seized Jason's frame. The suit he was wearing was ice and his skin had shrunk inside as far away from it as it could get.

"Oh my god!" Brad exclaimed. "You poor guy! You're freezing." He grabbed the bottle in the paper bag out of Jason's pocket, uncapped it and sniffed it. "Jesus! Cough syrup. You don't even have enough money for a decent bottle of Ripple!"

Jason couldn't have agreed with him more. Why had he brought cough syrup instead of Jack Daniels? The other drunks knew what to drink: they weren't shivering; some were even more scantily dressed than he, in shorts and undershirts.

"Honey, it's getting late," Moira said, "we gotta go."

"We can't leave him like this," Brad objected. He said suddenly, "Hey, no judgement, okay? But look—we're attending a college reunion in the hotel across the street. We got a room, too. Whyn't you come up to the room with us? Take a bath, get your clothes cleaned, get you something to eat. Hell, you could even spend the night with us, sleep on the couch."

"Wow, that sounds nice." Where the hell was that fool from the law firm? Jason stared wildly around. The number of men outside the store had thinned out, the circle of light from the store illuminated a broader stretch of empty sidewalk. Jason felt another shiver coming on.

"Yeah, come on." Brad's hand was on his arm, dragging him along. "Let's get out of the cold. I'm starting to freeze too."

Jason felt the resistance draining out of his body. It was getting easier to play along with the act, letting people do what they wanted to do with him. Maybe this was what it was like being homeless and a drunk, the slow erosion of willpower till you had none left at all. He felt himself being guided across the street to a tall building with a brightly lit lobby.

"Moira," Brad said, as the doorman came out to meet them, "you go in and get the key. I'll take Jason around to the loading-dock. Meet you at the apartment."

More darkness followed, a dim recess, a flight of stairs, doors, dim halls, more doors, mirrors, then a sudden silent uplift of gravity that came to a jolting halt.

Moments later Jason felt himself enveloped in the soothing confines of a uterine-like room: drapes, thick carpets, pillows, turned-down spreads, discrete pools of warming lamplight. The splash of water running into a tub came as he found himself hustled out of his clothes and wrapped in a robe. Moments later he was easing his chilled bones into warm bubbly water in the bright bathroom fogged with steam.

For what seemed like an eternity he closed his eyes and just floated. The bathroom door was open and he could hear the Bakers moving about, their low voices, keys rattling, doors opening and closing. A soapy floral smell rose around him in the steam.

This is nuts, he finally thought. What the fuck am I doing? I'm naked in a bathtub in a swanky hotel. This dream is going to pop and I'm going to find myself either on a gurney in an ambulance, or flat on my face in a puddle of vomit on the sidewalk.

Still he didn't move. He had no control over his body. It just wanted to lie there in physical bliss and he was powerless to make it do otherwise. Ever since he joined the crowd in front of the 7-Eleven, it seemed his resolve had been weakening. All his life he had had a single-minded determination to achieve some end, to arrive at some place. Now it seemed he lacked the ability to form even a velleity of a movement.

His troubles seemed a lifetime away, as though they belonged to someone else. This alone should have bothered him.

"How ya doing in there?" came Brad's voice from the other room. The TV was on, a news station. Moira's voice reached him again.

With a groan he lunged forward. He quickly washed himself and shampooed his hair. A glimpse of his rosy-skinned limbs greeted him as he pulled the embrace of a warmed towel around his shoulders. Another thought flitted through his mind: thank god I'm not rich. How would I ever get anything done?

As he was drying himself Brad's arm appeared in the door with a pile of clothes. "Gotcha some underwear," he said; "undershirt, shorts and socks."

"You didn't need to do that," Jason said.

"No problem."

He emerged moments later in the new underwear and a robe feeling simultaneously refreshed as though he had awakened from a deep sleep, and in control again. I'm going to tell them, he thought. I'll be my old self once I'm dressed again and I'll explain a little of what's been going on, why they happened to find me looking like a bum. They deserve the truth, even if it means I don't exactly need the help they're giving me. They didn't know that. Their hearts are in the right place.

# Chapter 8

"Hey, here he is!"

Brad stood there looking at him expectantly. Moira stood nearby, television remote in hand. They were both smiling but their eyes seemed to be looking out from behind the lower half of their faces and that part wasn't smiling. There was no sign of his clothes that were supposed to have been cleaned, but a large cardboard box sat between them on the bed.

"Have a drink?" Brad suggested suddenly, thrusting a glass toward him.

Jason waved it away. No one else had drinks and there appeared to be no other glasses in sight but the one he was being offered. "Thanks but no thanks. Let me just get dressed. I've got a confession to make, and you've already done more than enough for me."

"Well, we've sort of got a confession to make too, don't we Honey?"

"And you're more than welcome, Jason," Moira said, ignoring her husband's aside to her. "We're glad to be able to help."

"See, what happened was," Brad said, interposing himself slightly between Jason and the box on the bed, "was we weren't able to get your clothes cleaned, right Honey?"

"We sent them down to the laundry but they sent them back. They said they couldn't wash them, couldn't be responsible if anything happened to them."

"Well, that's too bad," Jason said. "I'll put them on the way they were."

"See, that's the problem," Brad said. "See, there's a men's shop in the lobby of the hotel. I noticed it was still open. We were going to buy you all new clothes, a new suit, new shoes, the works."

He beamed momentarily. "But uh, turns out that's a real high-end shop. Apparently they don't sell ready-to-wear clothes. You can't even buy a pair of pants down there without getting it hemmed first. That's where we got the underwear though."

"Okay, are those my old clothes in the box? Jason asked.

"Actually, that's what we're getting to, aren't we Honey? It turns out, there's a costume shop across the street. They were just closing."

"A costume shop?" Jason echoed.

"We got you a suit!" Moira said.

"That's right, they had one," Brad said.

Jason brightened again. "Oh, well let me see it."

Brad lifted the top off the box with a proud "Voila." Inside, on the folded clothes, sat a hat with a single long feather. Beneath it lay a folded chartreuse shirt, a pink polka-dot tie and a lavender coat and pair of pants.

"Come on," Brad said. "Let's get you into these and see how they fit. Medium tall's about your size, right?"

The pants were pleated and baggy except at the ankles where they had been pegged sharply. Brad helped pull them up under his armpits and cinched the belt. The coat reached down to his knees, its lapels wide enough to give lift to a 747, its shoulders padded enough to protect a line-backer. The tie was wide enough to land a 747. Only the shirt, with its overlarge collar, would have been acceptable under normal conditions, except for the color.

"This isn't a suit," Jason said, staring at himself in the mirror. "It's a *zoot* suit."

"That's what the salesman said," Moira parroted, as though amazed he'd been right.

"This goes with it," Brad said, attaching the watch-chain to Jason's belt loops. It hung down below the bottom of the coat.

The two-tone shoes were a little tight. Jason wiggled his toes. With the trousers tight around his ankles, it looked as though the whole whimsical confection had spewed out of the shoes like a chemistry experiment gone wrong. Jason stared at the outfit with horrified fascination. Still, sartorially speaking, it made more sense than a lot of other peoples' fashion choices.

"I can't wear this," he said finally. "I look like Jim Carrey. Give me my old clothes back."

"Well, that's the problem," Brad finally admitted. "We can't."

"What d'ya mean, *can't?*"

"We threw them away," Moira said.

"You threw my clothes away?"

"We were planning to buy you all new clothes. And we did, look. You can wear that. It looks great on you. All brand new. Never been worn."

"Your clothes couldn't be cleaned," Moira reminded him.

"I look—ridiculous!"

"Are the people at the 7-Eleven gonna care?"

"Come on," Moira said, "let's go downstairs. I'm starving."

"Yeah, come on," Brad urged. "We're missing the reception. All the food'll be gone. Not to mention the open bar.

"Put the hat back on," Brad said as they went out the door. "I love that feather!"

JASON SAT ALONE at a corner table behind a plate heaped with food that he now had little appetite for. The room was a bright, hanger-sized space full of balloons, people and tables. According to the placard at the door, three or four classes of Brad's college were being welcomed for the first of several days of get-togethers and activities.

A crowd around the band shuffled back and forth in unison. Doing the Electric Slide, he decided. Every now and then Brad or Moira drifted by, checking up on him. Every time Brad came by, he put the hat back on his head. Every now and then others stopped by, asked if they could join him, sat down, chatted, laughed and went away again, leaving their trash. Everybody loved his outfit.

The crowd on the dance floor were waving their arms now. Jason watched them spell out Y.M.C.A. Every table had a candle in the middle. If they turned out the lights, the atmosphere would have improved by a factor of a hundred. Something about the overbright environment seemed to drain the excitement from the crowd. Only those who were already drunk were in tune with the current in the room; the rest locked eyes with the gazes of their friends, contending against each other with muscular, sumo smiles.

He never did come clean with Brad and Moira about his homelessness act. The zoot suit they put him still rankled. They'd almost done it on purpose, it seemed, to humiliate him. He felt like a monkey in a circus. In fact, he had been on the point of angrily insisting Brad give him *his* clothes and wear the zoot suit himself. But the kindness of the suburban couple in trying to help kept his temper in check. Let them keep thinking he was the smartest kid in their class, the one who went to the best university in the Midwest, whose academic achievements were reported in the local paper, had somehow ended up on the streets. The thought of his real shortcomings carried him like a white-water stream out of the convention hall and back into the night.

The barriers in consciousness that put people in separate rooms wasn't in what people thought about, or the way they thought, he realized. It was what people *didn't* think about—that was what comprised the walls between them. He thought back to when he was a child and saw how the whole nation didn't think about black people; men on executive boards didn't think about women; nobody thought about gay people and he himself had never thought about Brad Baker till an hour ago.

People build their own chambers in consciousness to protect themselves. He could see that now. He looked out at the strangers around him and felt exposed, more unprotected in this outlandish costume than if he'd been wearing his own clothes, even his homelessness clothes. They at least said who he was; they kept intruders away. The lavender suit with the feather in the hat was a magnet for glances, for teasing or admiring comments.

The crowd around the band was surging again. People were falling in line. The line began winding between the tables. It was like a dragon at Chinese New Year that had had too much rice-wine. People were being conscripted into it, snatched from conversations, pulled out of their chairs.

Oh my god, Jason thought, it's headed this way. He stood abruptly and left.

# Chapter 9

Not much seemed to have changed outside except it was a little colder. The street was deserted except for the few remaining forms drifting like wingless moths in the glow of the 7-Eleven on the other side of the street, casting long shadows across the sidewalk under a burned-out street light.

Jason stood with his back to the lobby door under the marquee. The cold felt invigorating. He hadn't realized how hot it had gotten in the reception room.

Should he just leave? It had to be past one or two in the morning. He should say goodbye and a final thank-you to Brad and Moira first. They had stopped visiting his table at some point, he recalled. He would have to go back in and find them.

Glancing across at the 7-Eleven again, he wondered where his plan had gone wrong. Mr. Robin Wyatt had never shown up. Did Lindsey forget to call him? Sometimes when she was playing a new game she forgot what day it was. And then there was Luna. He had expected Luna would go out again; had she talked Lindsey into going with her?

It didn't matter now anyway. In a way it was good to be here, almost as if he'd stepped into a different world; the one he'd left behind was now almost too difficult to return to. Today was the day Donna was supposed to have started her job.

Air whooshed beside him and a woman walked out. Standing beside him, she fit a cigarette to her mouth, snapped a lighter and inhaled deeply.

"Hi," she said, noticing him at last.

Jason acknowledged her with a nod. She looked like she was doing the same thing he was, taking a break from the noise and the over-warm atmosphere. A pile of blond hair was pinned up in a youthful, contemporary mass but her face seemed to wear a permanently tired expression. She would get cold quickly in the dress she had on.

The next time she glanced at him, her gaze lingered on the clothes he was wearing.

"Going to a costume party?"

"No—"

"Just came from one?"

He shook his head again. "It's a long story."

"I like it. It's different." She drew on the cigarette a couple of times, then looked over again. "It's hot inside. Feels good out here."

He nodded. The smell of her smoke was rich and pungent. It reminded him how much he loved the smell of a new pack of cigarettes. He used to carry a freshly-opened pack in his shirt pocket, to strengthen his will-power, when he was trying to quit.

"What's your name?" she asked.

"Jason," he said.

"Hi Jason. My name's Candice."

"Hi, Candice."

"Want to go upstairs?"

"Upstairs—?"

"Yes, to my room." A note of impatience edged her voice.

Jason smiled. "No thanks."

She looked away, combining a shrug, a shiver, a twirl of the cigarette and an inhalation in one movement.

"How 'bout a drink?" he countered.

"No" she said, crushing the cigarette under her heel. The door whooshed again and she was gone.

Across the street the streetlight on the corner by the 7-Eleven suddenly clicked on again.

Jason turned to watch the woman cross the lobby as though she herself had somehow turned the light on from inside. The tap of her determined steps faded as she disappeared toward the reception room. He was feeling the cold again now. Waiting so as to not follow Candice too closely, he finally went in himself.

More people were standing now around the dance floor and among the littered tables. Someone had finally dimmed the lights and a disco ball was spinning. Scattered constellations whirled over the crowd as though someone had rolled the cosmos into a ball and given it a kick, making it harder now to identify individual faces.

At one of the tables stood a few people around the form of a woman with her head on its surface, her hair spread among the dishes of half-eaten food, ashtrays, coffee cups and glasses. As he approached, the group turned to look at him hopefully.

"Moira?" he said, recognizing the shawl and patterned dress she was wearing. "What happened?"

"She fell off her chair," one of the women said. "We just saw her." Someone else said, "somebody should probably take her up to her room, if she has one—or home."

"Where's her husband, Brad?" Jason asked.

Shrugs and silence met his question. "I take it you're not her husband," one of them said.

"No, I'm a friend," he said.

Moira suddenly sat upright. "I have to pee," she said thickly.

Jason brushed a cigarette butt and pieces of food out of her hair. "I'll take care of her," he said. "Is her purse here?"

With expressions of gratitude, the good Samaritans began drifting away. Someone placed her purse on the table and picked up her shawl.

"Wheresh Brad," Moira said, starting to lean again.

"I don't know, but you should go upstairs and go to bed." Jason rooted through her purse which contained nothing but a tampon, a compact, a lipstick and a pack of gum, located her key-card and put the rest back.

"My hushband's a bashturd," she said. She angled her woozy eyes up at Jason. "Are you a bashturd too?"

"All men are bashturds," He said, imitating her pronunciation. "Can you stand?"

"Leamme 'lone," she said, collapsing on the table again.

He hauled her to her feet and got under an arm. "Don't puke on my zoot suit," he warned, steering her toward the door.

As though the magic word had been spoken, her body began heaving.

Jason dropped her back and after a moment the heaving subsided and her eyes began closing again.

Looking about for another way to get her up, his eye fell on her shawl. Peacocks in shimmery colors emblazoned its surface, their feathers blending into its fringe. He used it to tie her to her chair.

"Alright," he said, "let's try that again."

Tilting her back, he dragged her a few feet, then, satisfied she wouldn't immediately topple over, he turned around and pulled the chair from behind, travois-style.

As he started toward the elevators, picking up speed across the smoother lobby floor, a bell-hop appeared and lifted the front legs. Together they got her up to her room. Raising her carefully they laid her and the chair on the bed. She was still tied to it.

"Here, here . . . " Jason cast about for a tip as the bell-hop lingered. He had no money and there was none in Moira's purse. Something gold caught his eye: Brad's watch, lying among the things he had left on the dresser. Jason thrust it into the bell-hop's hands. "Here, take this. Thanks!"

Jason looked down at the sleeping woman after the bell-hop left. With her limbs sprawled and her hair spread mop-like across the pillow and eyeliner running down her scarlet cheeks, she resembled a captured maenad—a middle-aged, suburban bacchante. All the skills desperate older women employ to make themselves look young were smeared on her face, as though she had fallen onto a palette of magic poultices.

It wasn't that she wasn't attractive anymore, but that her thinking was so obviously divided about herself, that her face was a blur of two images, one the forty-year-old woman that was her chronological self, the other the twenty-year-old girl she still felt herself to be. Each true at the same time, yet in separate spaces.

Still afraid she might vomit, he made no effort to untie her, but taking the bedspread that had been folded down he pulled it over her and tucked her in. Then going into the sitting-room, he turned on the TV and dropped into a chair.

The windows were still dark, but a nervous system long accustomed to measuring the hours of the night told him it had to be getting close to dawn. He drooped in the chair, the events of the night reeling about his brain. A reluctance to leave till he had thanked Brad and said his goodbyes kept him immobile.

He must have dozed off because the sound of the door opening and closing startled him upright. Brad stood there unsteadily, coat over his arm, shirt unbuttoned.

"Where's Moira?"

"In there." He nodded toward the bedroom. No need to whisper. Moira would be out for a while.

"Whoa, lookit that!" Brad cried suddenly, catching sight of the TV.

Jason focused on the image that was floating before him;

or rather 'images' since there seemed to be about ten of them, all body parts tangled up and moving rhythmically together.

"Shit, I'm watching porn," he said.

"Yeah, man!"

"Where've you been?" he said, sharply clicking the set off. "It's almost morning. Moira was looking for you."

Brad chuckled. His voice dropped into a guys-only groove that sounded more like a schoolboy with a girly magazine. "I got a new friend. Her name's Candice. We've been hanging out together, if you know what I mean."

"Oh—Candice," Jason said.

"You know her?"

"By now I think every man in the hotel knows her."

"You think I shouldn't have gone up to her room?"

"I didn't say that."

"Ya think hookin' up w' some lonely divorcee at a convention or somewhere's cheatin'?"

"Everyone wants to have an adventure," Jason said. "Some find more adventure close to home than they can handle."

"Whatsa harm, s'long's wife doesn't know?"

"May be too late for that," he said, recalling Moira's verbal dexterity with a certain two-syllable epithet. He got to his feet. "I gotta get outa here. It's late."

"Hey, don't run off so soon. Let's have a drink." Brad fumbled with a line-up of miniatures on the refrigerator and uncapped one. When Jason waved him away, Brad shrugged, uncapped the second as well, downed it, pulled a chair out from under the table and stumbled into it.

Jason watched his face contort as the liquor went down. Slices of shadow and lamp-light seemed to pull at his features. Had Brad always been this ugly? Brad had changed. Even when his face fell back into its customary grooves, Jason saw now something out of alignment, something whose pieces no longer fit.

Brad's face too, like Moira's, showed the effects of the passing of time—but it wasn't advancing age. Everything in their lives showed it; they were in different worlds. They had drifted apart, but somehow still connected enough for each to know the suffering of the other. Brad had become untrustworthy, Moira unappealing.

Jason's own life flashed before his eyes. Time works through consciousness too. How many times had he himself been in that incandescent oneness with another person, who today would be a stranger if he met her again?

You can't stand still in consciousness. He saw that now. This crazy escapade his friendship with Donna had propelled him into, if it had done anything at all, had shown him he had to keep going. Consciousness was no stronger than a soap-bubble in a high wind, and he was a drifter.

"Heck yeah," Brad was saying, smacking his lips, "We used to follow everything you did in college."

"Yeah, well, I got something I need to do," he said.

"The Loveland Daily Register printed every semester you made the Dean's List," Brad said, "the sports you tried out for, when you graduated summa . . . I can still see it now: Local Boy Does Good."

"I did okay in college," Jason agreed. "I got to take classes in all kinds of subjects. It wasn't till I got to grad school that I ran into trouble."

"Nobody wrote about *my* exploits in college, all the teams *I* was on," Brad said sadly.

"And look at us now," Jason said. "You the successful businessman, me wearing a zoot suit."

"Yeah, look at us now."

"Well, I got things to do," he repeated.

"Hey, doan mention anything to Moira about Candice, okay. Thass just between old friends, okay?"

"Sure. My lips are sealed."

"Well, iss been nice catchin' up with ya."

"Yeah, you too. You guys are the greatest." He patted the lapels of the coat he had on. "Thanks again for the suit. I'm starting to like it. —Oh, by the way." He paused at the door. "One of the bell-hops helped me get Moira into bed. I couldn't find any money to tip him with, so I gave him your watch."

"My watch?" Brad gripped his bare wrist, then looked at the top of the dresser.

"I hope it wasn't too expensive."

"It was a Rolex. You gave 'im my Rolex?" Brad repeated.

"Yeah. So long, guy! See you in another ten years."

Jason closed the door quietly and took the stairs down.

# Chapter 10

It turned out the offices of Caspar and Caspar were right around the corner; but to get there, he had to first remember where he parked the car, get Robin Wyatt's card out and look up the address on his phone, Mapquest it, decide to leave his car where it was because in another hour there wouldn't be any place to park downtown, walk back, remember that it still wasn't even seven o'clock yet and the firm probably wouldn't open till eight, and end up back at the hotel, sitting at a window in the coffee-shop with a cup of coffee and a doughnut in front of him.

From here he had an excellent view of the sun rising into the pearly sky, the street filling with people and cars. The scene was like a medieval triptych: heaven at the top, the towering facades of purgatory in the middle and the damned at the bottom, pouring out of buses, running up from underground garages and subways, or stuck in their cars on the

grid-locked streets, not even able to get out and take a piss, bur-
dened with the accoutrements of their suffering, newspapers,
coffee cups, lunches and brief-cases, shoving into the inevitably
too-small doors of the indifferent buildings, their windows already beginning to blaze.

His gaze lingered on the luminescent roses and salmons of
the sky and the evolving blue of morning-glories above them.
Why couldn't people live on the tops of the buildings, he
thought. They could come down into the hell of a new day
every morning, rise up through the purgatories of the buildings
during the day, and return to heaven in the evening. They would
watch the sun set and the sun rise and sleep under the stars at
night.

Soon he too would ascend into one of the buildings of purgatory. Today was the day he would find out what he'd been
hiding from for the past week. Today was also the day Donna
would start a new job or not start a new job, and Gina would
get her fired or not get her fired. Donna had said she was supposed to start at a coffee-shop in a downtown hotel; he looked
around and thought, no, not this coffee-shop. A better coffee-
shop in a better hotel, maybe the St Regis or Four Seasons. It
would have to be the kind of place that would make sure you
never got another waitressing job in a good hotel in the city
again.

He splashed water on his face in the restroom, combed his
hair and settled the hat with the long feather back on his head—
not because it belonged with the costume that was the only
thing he had to wear, but out of a half-formed superstition that
the get-up had somehow kept him out of trouble the night be-

fore, that without it, for some reason he couldn't explain, he might well have taken Candice up on her invitation. Standing there, meeting the calculating gaze she trained on him, he had had that feeling you feel that makes you want to grab a hand-rail. The suit had steadied him.

The resplendence of the offices of Caspar and Casper were visible the moment you stepped off the elevator. Plate-glass walls framed double mahogany doors opening into the hall on the top floor of an historic Art Deco building. If you were the plaintiff, you would feel the gods were on your side before you even crossed the threshold; if the defendant, the will to resist would evaporate.

Quelling the urge to turn around and go home, Jason pulled the door open and presented himself at the reception-ist's desk.

Lights blinked on the phone but no one was on duty. It was still early, fifteen past eight. Suddenly a young woman came rushing out, coffee in one hand and a pastry in the other. Pushing buttons, speaking hurriedly, scribbling notes, she finally punched one last button and said pertly, "Mr. Er-ickson on line two, sir."

"Hi, I'm Jason Rocketts," Jason said when she finally looked up at him. "Is Robin Wyatt here? I got a message he's looking for me."

She took the card he held out without taking her eyes off his suit. It alone seemed to tell her all she needed to know about who he was.

"Jason Rocketts is here, sir," she said, punching another button. Repeating "Yes, sir," three times in a row, she hung up, handed the card back and said, "Please have a seat, Mr. Rocketts. Mr. Caspar will be with you shortly."

The reception area was big enough to do laps in, and Jason did several. Something wouldn't let his body bend enough to sit down, though the leather couches and chairs looked inviting. He studied the Currier and Ives prints on the wall instead, soothing himself with images of sleigh-riding and harvesting in an unreal America of the past.

"Mr. Rocketts? This way, please."

Another young woman. After leading him through a labyrinth of halls, she ushered him into a well-appointed conference room. A huge mahogany table occupied its center, surrounded by comfortable-looking swivel-back chairs. Several miles of books on wooden shelves covered the walls, grouped by nation and tribe: all the black with red lettering on one shelf, blue with silver lettering on another; a whole wall of gray with gold lettering looked too powerful to even read.

Dad had wanted him to be a lawyer. He recalled his dad's smell, sweat, hair tonic and the sour mixture of cigarette smoke and alcohol on his breath. The man had never gone to college, but he'd had a good head for figures. He'd started out selling insurance, a door-to-door salesman.

People looked down on him because he only had a high school education, but he'd done pretty well for himself. He'd left his wife a rich widow. A man could do worse than start at the bottom and work his way up.

What was it he used to say, whenever the subject of college came up? Dad loved those pithy little sayings he got out of greeting cards. "Dogs don't eat dogs."

A grunt of laughter lightened his mood. "What did he mean, 'Dogs don't eat dogs'? Of course dogs ate dogs. A wolf will run you down, and Fido'll scavenge you."

Half-baked, that was his Dad. Why he couldn't stay out of trouble.

But almost immediately the door opened again and a thin gray-faced man and a younger man in a bowtie and short-sleeved dress shirt entered. The younger man guided the older one to a chair opposite and pushed him into it.

"So," the younger man said, sitting down himself, "you're the one pretending to be Jason Rocketts."

Jason stiffened as though someone had dropped a viper in front of him. "I *am* Jason Rocketts," he said, frowning.

"I suppose you have some ID?" the younger man prodded.

Jason reached for his back pocket—and stopped. His wallet was in the car. All he had on him was Robin Wyatt's business card. He pulled it out instead.

"I don't know who you think Jason Rocketts is, but I'm here to see Robin Wyatt. I got a message he wanted to see me." He tossed the card across the table. "He'll tell you who I am."

"*I'm* Robin Wyatt," the young man said, his Adam's apple waving as he lifted his chin. "And you're *not* Jason Rocketts."

He tossed the card back and stared at him challengingly.

Jason looked hard now at the gray-faced man beside Robin. Something about the man seemed familiar. His sunken cheeks appeared to have been hurriedly shaved, leaving his face with reddish patches. The pink shirt with its white collar, the same two-tone style Robin Wyatt wore, spread open to reveal a bony neck; both that and the fitted suit he was wearing were several sizes too small. The shirt cuffs barely reached his wrist-bones and the sleeves of the coat, stylishly cut above the cuffs, were almost at his elbows. The man struggled to keep his hands off the table-top. When they appeared, they shook like egg-beaters.

At that moment the door at the other end opened and an older man appeared. He threw a folder on the table and dropped into a chair.

"So," he said. "Will the real Jason Rocketts please stand up?"

The gray-faced man jumped to his feet, looking terrified. Robin Wyatt pulled him down again.

"I don't know what's going on," Jason said, "but I got a message Robin Wyatt was trying to get in touch with me, so here I am." He proffered the card again.

The older man looked at Jason, apparently seeing him for the first time. His eyes narrowed faintly as if to bring into focus what it was he was looking at. Seemingly he had never seen a zoot suit before. Finally he glanced down over his granny glasses at the card, then pushed it back.

"He's lying. He's not Jason Rocketts. *This* is Jason Rocketts!" Robin gave the man a shove that almost knocked him out of his chair.

Jason opened his mouth to protest but Robin wasn't finished yet.

"Ask him if he has any ID."

"My wallet's in my car," Jason admitted.

"Can you run down and get it?" the older man asked.

"My car's actually a couple blocks away. I didn't park in the garage."

Mr. Caspar leaned his forehead on the edge of the folder. Finally he said, "I don't have all day for this . . . Alright, here's what we do." The folder slapped down on the table again. "We'll play twenty questions."

"Excuse me, but before we do anything, can somebody tell me what this is all about? I might not *want* to play twenty questions."

"It's about Mrs. Rocketts."

"What about her?"

"I'm sorry. Privileged information. That's all I can tell you. Only if you're her son can I tell you more. So," he added, "you in or not?"

My god, when is this going to end? Jason thought. This is insane.

"Fine. First question," Mr. Caspar said; "I'll make it an easy one. What is your mother's first name?"

"Judeen," the gray faced man said quickly; "Judelyn, Gerrilynn," he amended twice as Robin spoke in his ear.

"Gerrilynn's right," Jason said.

"Good. Next question. Your mother's net worth is what, one million, five million or ten million?"

Again Robin whispered into his companion's ear. "Five million."

"I don't know," Jason said. "I don't know what her net worth is. I don't know anything about her finances."

"O-kay," Mr. Caspar said. "Another easy one. Where was your mother born?"

"St Paul, St Cloud . . . St Something. It begins with a 'Saint'," Jason said.

"St Louis," the gray faced man said.

"Correct."

"Well I was close," Jason muttered. "I got the first part right."

"Not close enough," Robin said.

"Next question. Listen up. What year were your mother and father married?"

This appeared to stump even the tag-team of Robin and friend. A thorny silence settled over the table. Finally Robin's mouth moved again at his companion's ear.

"Nineteen Thirty Five," the gray faced man blurted.

"Correct," Mr. Caspar said.

"Now how would I remember something like that?" Jason said.

The older man looked over disapprovingly. "Would you happen to remember your own mother's birthday, by chance?"

"I haven't been in touch with my mother for forty years. How would I remember her birthday? She never remembered mine."

"January 3rd, Nineteen Nineteen," the gray faced man said.

"*He* doesn't know squat about my mother," Jason finally exploded. "Your employee's coaching him. Send him out of the room and ask your question."

"Very good," Mr. Caspar approved, ignoring Jason's outburst. "Next question. In what year were your mother and father indicted for wire and bank fraud."

"Nineteen Forty One."

"I wasn't even born then," Jason said. "How would I know that? Besides, the charges were dropped." He remembered again Dad's favorite saying and felt a stab of pity.

"One last question," Mr. Caspar announced. "Only Gerrilynn Rocketts' real son could know this." He cleared his throat, a sound that seemed to draw everyone closer. "How did your mother sleep, in a nightgown, or in the nude?"

The tag-team conferred and the gray faced man said triumphantly, "in the nude!"

"How the fuck would *anyone* know that—except her husband?" Jason demanded. "And how would a mother's son know how his mother sleeps, unless he'd been in bed with her too?"

Mr. Caspar lowered the file he had been toying with and pointed across the table. "Get that drunk out of here," he snapped. "And Robin—I'll see *you* in my office."

# Chapter 11

The intensive care unit of Suburban General Hospital was thrumming with life. Jason had to pause, coming into it from the quiet and relatively dark halls of the rest of the building. Its brightness was magnified by the light reflecting from the glass walls of what seemed like a hundred cubicles, its noise a chorus of voices, wheezing and beeping machines, overhead announcements and various other incomprehensible ringings and buzzings pitched to instill alarm in even a visitor.

You couldn't even stand still to take it all in: incessant cries of "Excuse us, look out, coming through" kept you off balance as a constant tide of people, gurneys and wheel-chairs surged in different directions. No matter where you stood, you were always in the way.

Somewhere in this maelstrom was a woman in a coma.

After signing papers in the offices of Caspar and Caspar that morning to terminate the life of an old woman who he was surprised to learn had lived within a dozen miles of him for the past ten years, the least he could do, he decided, was to go out and visit her, to say a final farewell, albeit a one-sided one.

Lindsey, whom he had awakened after a night hanging out with their new roommate, had declined the ritual, saying instead, "she won't know I'm not there. You can say good-bye for both of us. I need my shut-eye."

"Why didn't anyone tell me a week ago what you wanted?" Jason had complained when Mr. Caspar told him, after Robin Wyatt and his friend had exited the room, that Jason held his mother's power of attorney for health care, and the hospital needed his agreement to pull the plug on her life-support.

"If we'd put an ad in the paper, can you imagine how many Jason Rocketts' would have shown up? Besides, privacy is one of the services we guarantee our clients. Your mother was a very private person."

Gerrilynn Rocketts was also a very lonely person. Her only remaining next of kin hadn't had any contact with her for twenty years. The servants had vanished after carrying off almost everything in the house that wasn't nailed down. It was the neighbors who finally noticed her mail wasn't being picked up. She was found on the floor of her bathroom in a drying puddle of urine. All this had happened six months ago.

Jason had listened to this without a twinge of emotion. The papers were brought in to sign; after retrieving and presenting his driver's license, the notary signed and the matter was settled. Gerrilynn's life support would be turned off at noon the next day. Funeral arrangements had already been made.

While he was waiting for the elevator for the last time, finally leaving to go home, Robin Wyatt appeared. Ignoring him, he occupied himself urging the floor lights to move faster. Jason noticed he had a plant, framed photos of himself and a collection of hair care products in a box he was carrying.

As they were going down Jason finally broke the silence. "You found that guy who was pretending to be me from the 7-Eleven around the corner, didn't you?"

"I got pranked," Robin said, looking defiantly at a spot on the elevator wall.

"What d'ya mean?"

"A woman called me up and told me you wanted to meet me there." His hands occupied holding the box, the rest of his body fidgeted.

That wasn't the message he'd asked Lindsey to relay. Had she gotten it wrong, or had Robin misunderstood?

"When you weren't there, I thought, well, two can play this game."

"I thought he looked familiar. How much did you offer him?" In the meantime he was wondering why he hadn't thought of sending an impersonator himself, to find out what they wanted.

"A hundred."

"Did you give it to him?"

"I let him keep my suit."

A few more people got on. "I'm glad it happened." Robin

lifted his chin and looked at the air defiantly. "I was going to quit anyway."

A pang of remorse hit Jason. "Maybe it as just a mistake."

"I know when I've been pranked," Robin said bitterly. Moments later, as the elevator stopped again, he said, "Fuck that tight-assed old queen Chuckie Caspar and his trick questions!"

As they went out onto the sidewalk, he said before disappearing in the crowd, "don't feel sorry for me. I've got a job in design waiting for me. People have been begging me to take it for months now."

NOW JASON SET OUT to find his mother's cubicle alone. He had stood as close as he could get to the nurses' station without being asked what he wanted. And having stopped at home to change first, hanging the zoot suit carefully in his closet in case he ever needed it again—or got invited to a party—there was less reason for the harried staff to notice him.

Fortunately on the wall of each cubicle the nurses had tapped the patient's name; some were on restrictions, others at risk for falls or were highly contagious, and these alerts too were tapped nearby.

Every cubicle had a life-form in it, though in one it lay flat on the bed with a sheet over its head; the lights were out and all the machines silent and dark; but for the most part they held still-living people, or rather the rinds of people, the physical residue of lifetimes of thoughts and feelings, of

dreams and anguishes, the bloodless coals of a lifetime of deci-
sions and evasions, kept alive by the machines with their bags
of fluids that dripped into their veins and the tubes that
breathed into their lungs.

In one a patient sat up and ate from a tray, in another a patient was out of bed, sitting in a chair, surrounded by a forest
of life-supporting poles with their bags of fruit, in another a tor-
nado of medical personnel whirled about a bed while machines
screamed in terror and tried to drive them away with their jerk-
ing lines, in another visitors silently gathered.

Finally he reached the sign that read, 'Gerrilynn Rocketts'.
Under that it said 'Blue Team'. Under that was another sign
that read:

## TO BE RESUSCITATED

Jason had no idea what to expect when he entered the cubicle. He hadn't seen his mother in forty years. His last image
of her was of a woman in full possession of her powers, arm
bangles, ear-rings, lustrous hair regally coiffed about her temples
without a strand of gray, scarlet, beak-like lips, imperious eyes
that looked at you as though all the snakes of the Gorgon's head
were struggling to get out through her pupils.

What met his gaze now was no different from any of the
other bloodless rinds in the other cubicles of the ICU. A body
the size of a child, the bone of an arm, skin whiter than the
sheets, hair reduced to a few gray streaks over a hairless scalp,
tubes taped to the nose and mouth, running into each arm and
under the sheet, a bag stuffed with yellow fluid hanging from

the side of the bed. A TV set's somnolent murmur under-scored the atmosphere's lethal tranquility.

Jason looked down at the patient in the bed. Outside the window, low clouds hung over a land stripped of color, leafless boughs interlacing in a hedge against the oncoming winter. Crows in the distance traced their simulacrums of the vari-able winds but no winds were blowing.

The only discordant note was the three of them on the bedside stand, himself, Lindsey and Dad, looking completely sober, in a framed photograph that must have been taken in the Sixties. They stood staring into the sun, as normal a family as they could have been, Lindsey in the middle, close to each other but not touching. No doubt courtesy of a neighbor.

Parents are just like other people, he thought; if we don't know them, they're strangers to us. Our being their children gives us the most intimate look at their personal lives possible, but beyond that—if the relationship isn't kept up, they're nothing. Passengers on the Titanic share more meaningful memories than parents and children. Lindsey was right not to have bothered to come.

This was not some lack of feeling to be deplored. He would have cared more if the patient had been an old woman trying to cross a busy street. I would still choose you and Dad, he thought, if I could choose my parents in the next life; my only hope would be that you and Dad would be happier with each other, and with your children. But he was swearing fealty to a pair of statues dug out of an excavation. If he came back in the next life, he wanted to come back as himself, but with a happier childhood.

"Well," he said aloud at last, addressing the island of silence in the hospital bed, "you've been living only a few miles from us but you never got in touch with us. And we never tried to get in touch with you. I guess you were never meant to have children, and I at least was never meant to have parents.

"Anyway, Lindsey says hi. She's doing well. And I'm still hanging in there. Tomorrow they're going to disconnect you, so I guess this is goodbye."

At that moment the clouds, through which patches of permissive blue were still showing, suddenly jostled, igniting the space between them with a golden fire. The edges of the clouds, like the edges of paper in a fire, curled up in flame. A beam lit up the cubicle, touching everything in its path as if to grasp whatever was not fastened down and pull it out to itself.

People were like polyps in their calcified corals of consciousnesses, he thought; if only they could let go, embrace the column of water that surrounded them, lose themselves in the translucence that is the soul of their existence, then perhaps the world would come alive again, the body and soul of the world would also become one, its missing dimension of emotion return.

He turned the TV off, turned off the light, tore the 'Resuscitate' sign off the wall and left.

# Chapter 12

Rain was falling in patches on the earth. Jason had been awake for about forty-eight hours. For a man who spent most of his awake life driving at night, the daylight proved tricky. Cars appeared to be turning in front of him when they were only changing lanes; overpasses appeared lower than they actually were. The grainy mixture of rain and no-rain, of light and no-light, seemed about to get him killed.

Nevertheless, a force greater than himself turned the wheel of the car toward one final stop. Steering into the narrower streets of the city was somewhat of a relief. He was a pilot bringing his craft to a landing, guided by streetlights, their colors honed by the rain, like lights on a runway.

A beam of light had drawn him out; that was the only way he could express it. It had lit up a path for him; but this was no 'Idea' like the rest of his ideas. This experience called him to follow it; the first idea he'd ever had that demanded a response.

It would also be the first idea he never told anyone. Before he even took a step, that part of his life closed. The light that lit up a path for him had also illuminated his life. No longer could he live only for himself, using friends as an audience, seeking to expand himself into their lives, his thoughts into their heads. He would live now as a therapist, listening, opening himself to *their* lives. It would not shrink him to fill his life with others.

Arriving at his destination, he parked in a handicapped space. Some things never change he thought as he exited the car and walked up to the building with the nondescript façade. More cars get ticketed in good weather than in bad, he'd observed. Anyway, he didn't plan to stay long.

First he walked down the main hall and knocked on the wall where Donna's kitchen would be, then came back and knocked on her door. Hearing this, she would know it was him.

Instead of appearing in her painting clothes, the door was opened by a woman in a bathrobe, hair tousled, face-jewelry missing.

Donna squinted out at him. "What's up?"

"Did I wake you?" he said.

"It was a late night. I can't let you in. Gina's still sleeping.

"I guess you didn't start your job," he said.

A shadow of a scowl appeared. She shook her head.

"What happened?"

"You've got some nerve, asking me that."

"I'm still a friend, aren't I? Whether you like me or not."

"I decided to give Gina another chance," she said tiredly. "What else could I do? We're going to start couple's counseling."

"Well, is that a bad thing?"

"I guess not. It's good to have someone. —At least I don't have to *pay* people to hang out with me."

A bitter expression flashed as the door was being closed. Then it latched quietly.

At some level of reality the door had kept coming and hit him in the face. A pang shot through his heart.

A moment later the door opened again.

"I'm sorry," Donna said. "That was uncalled for." A penitent expression softened her face. "I don't know what came over me, but I know you did your best."

The light brightened in her eyes and seemed to dance toward his face. "You know—you and I were almost a couple. Once."

"That was a long time ago," he said.

"It was, wasn't it? I'm glad things turned out like they did. I like it better this way." She glanced quickly inside, then stepped out and stood on her toes. Her face filled his gaze as her lips lightly touched his.

"At least I've outlasted all the other men in your life," he said as she withdrew behind her door again.

"Indeed you have," she said, closing it softly. "Indeed you have . . . "

www.ingramcontent.com/pod-product-compliance
Lightning Source LLC
Chambersburg PA
CBHW030534020726
47494CB00004B/1354

* 9 7 8 1 7 3 2 2 8 8 2 4 9 *